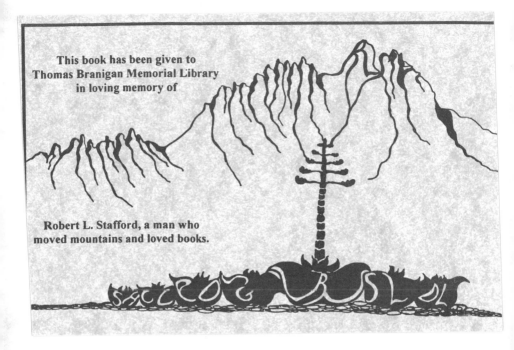

This book has been given to
Thomas Branigan Memorial Library
in loving memory of

Robert L. Stafford, a man who
moved mountains and loved books.

Woman Slaughter

By E. X. Ferrars

E · X · FERRARS

Woman Slaughter

DOUBLEDAY
New York London Toronto Sydney Auckland

PUBLISHED BY DOUBLEDAY
a division of Bantam Doubleday Dell Publishing Group, Inc.
666 Fifth Avenue, New York, New York 10103

DOUBLEDAY and the portrayal of an anchor
with a dolphin are trademarks of Doubleday,
a division of the Bantam Doubleday Dell Publishing Group, Inc.

Library of Congress Cataloging-in-Publication Data

Ferrars, E. X.
    Woman slaughter/E.X. Ferrars.—1st ed. in U.S.A.
        p. cm.
    I. Title.
PR6003.R458W6   1990
823'.912—dc20   89-25971
CIP

ISBN 0-385-26491-7

Woman Slaughter

ONE

I HAD OPENED my front door to go out and post some letters when my telephone rang. I turned and went to answer it, leaving the door standing open, and that was how I heard the squeal of brakes, the hoarse scream, and the frenzied yelping of a dog.

I left the telephone to ring and in fact never discovered who it was who had tried to call me then. It could even have been a wrong number. I ran back to the door and out into the road and saw a car disappearing down it and vanishing out of sight at the corner.

The evening was very foggy, so all I saw was that it was a big car and the gleam of its rear-lights. I also saw something dark lying in the road. The yelping of the dog went on.

I ran towards that dark object which lay there so still. At the same time several other people erupted from houses nearby and ran towards it.

"Oh God!" someone cried. "It's Mr. Creed."

"An ambulance," someone else said. It was my next-door neighbour, Mrs. Bulpitt. "Quick—you go, Mrs. Freer."

"But he's—he's dead, he's been killed," someone said.

"The devil, the wicked devil!" Mrs. Bulpitt exclaimed.

"Perhaps knocking the poor old man down wasn't his fault. Mr. Creed may have wandered out in front of him in this fog. It's the kind of thing he'd do. But not to stop . . . !"

She was a small, fierce-looking woman of about sixty. In the light from the street-lamps her little withered face looked tense with anger rather than with mere shock at the disaster. She had been living in the house next to mine for about two years and we saw a fair amount of one another. I knew that she was liable to take charge of any situation in which she found herself.

"That poor dog," one of the neighbours said. "He's hurt too."

But the dog was not dead, for now its yelping had become an eerie howl.

However, I did not wait to find out what had happened to the poor animal, but made for my door and my telephone, which by then had stopped ringing.

I dialled 999, demanded an ambulance, and then on second thoughts asked for the police too.

When I was connected with the police station I said that there had been what looked like a fatal accident in Ellsworthy Street, and gave my name and address. Then I returned to the scene in the road.

A small crowd had at first gathered closely around the figure that lay there so dreadfully still; they had now withdrawn some paces from it, as if, their first curiosity satisfied, or their compassion recognized to be useless, the fact of death was something from which it was impossible not to shrink back. They were muttering among themselves, asking one another if they had really seen nothing, had not seen where the car had come from or what kind of car it was.

A woman had picked up the dog, an old rough-haired foxterrier, and was stroking it and softly crooning to it. Its howling had ceased.

She gave me a surprisingly bright smile.

"I don't believe he's hurt at all," she said. "Just frightened."

She was plainly one of the people to whom a possibly injured dog was more important than the corpse of a man. An old man, Mr. Creed, who had lived in the house just opposite to mine.

It was at that moment that I remembered that his wife was in hospital and realized that someone, someone who might well be me, would have to break the news of this tragedy to her, unless the police would take it on themselves. Malcolm and Julia Creed were old friends of mine. They had been living in Ellsworthy Street even before I had come to live there, as I had when my mother died, leaving her house to me. That had happened soon after my marriage had broken up and I had been very glad of somewhere to settle, particularly as I had been able to get some part-time work in my old job as a physio-therapist in a clinic in the town of Allingford.

"He must have been out walking his dog as he always did about now," Mrs. Bulpitt said. "I expect he just walked out from between all these cars right in front of whoever was driving. I often saw him hesitating on the pavement before crossing, then he'd suddenly dart out when he ought to have stayed still. He never got used to how much traffic there is along here now."

She was probably right. In the days when Malcolm and Julia Creed had come to live there, Ellsworthy Street had been very quiet. Most of the houses along it were semi-detached Victorian, with what had once been carriage-houses but now were garages, so that there had been very little need for parking in the street. But now half the people who lived

there had at least two cars, and the people who lived in one
of the streets into which Ellsworthy Street led, a street where
there were no garages and which nowadays was very busy,
had discovered that it was very convenient for parking. So
both sides of the street, by the evening, were usually lined
with cars, and neither Mr. Creed nor his dog had ever become accustomed to the change.

But it suddenly occurred to me that there had been no cars
parked in front of Mrs. Bulpitt's house when I had heard the
cry, the yelping of the dog, and the squeal of brakes. I had
not thought about it till that moment, but now I glanced
towards the house. In the cars parked almost stem to stern
along the street there was a gap in front of it as well as in
front of mine. Yet someone had just parked his car not simply
in front of my house, where it would not have mattered, but
in front of the entrance to my garage.

It made me angry. Not that I wanted to take my car out
that evening, but perhaps the newly arrived car would still be
there in the morning, when I knew that I should want to go
out. Anyway, it was something that ought not to have been
done. I believe that the nervous state I was in made me even
angrier than I should have been normally. If there had not
been so much else on my mind at the time, I should have
strode up to the driver before he had time to vanish and told
him none too courteously that he could not leave his car
where it was.

But then something about the driver struck me. He was
not moving away, but was standing beside his car, looking at
the group of people in the road. There was a street-lamp near
him, its light falling on his fair hair, his pale, nearly triangular
face, and his strange bright eyes.

I went up to him quickly.

"Felix!" I said.

He was my one-time husband, Felix Freer, with whom I had parted nearly seven years before, after a marriage which had somehow managed to survive for three. But it was nothing like seven years since I had last seen him. We had never taken the trouble to have a divorce and we still met from time to time; as long as this did not happen too often and the meetings did not last for too long, our relationship stayed fairly amicable. It seemed to me that our meetings tended to happen when there was something that I could do for him, but perhaps he thought that there were times when I made use of him. He could be useful sometimes, because he was really a very clever man and in his way was helpful and good-natured. If only he had been able to tell the truth at least some of the time, which unfortunately was not a habit of his, I believe I might have been able somehow to patch our marriage together.

"What's happened, Virginia?" he asked, looking along the road.

"An old man, an old friend of mine, has been knocked down by a car and killed," I said. "The car didn't stop."

He gave a nod. "I thought that was it."

"You mean you saw it?"

"I saw something. I saw a car do a wild swerve in the road, then go off like a bat out of hell. Then I saw all you people come running out and that—it's an old man, you said—that old man lying in the road."

"Did you see the number of the car?"

I was not sure if he hesitated.

"No," he said.

"Did you see if it was driving along the road ahead of you, or was it parked somewhere here?" I asked.

"I'm not sure. I wasn't paying much attention till I saw it do the swerve. What brought all you people out?"

"I heard a scream and the dog yelping. I knew something was wrong. I suppose that's what the other people heard too."

He put an arm round me, kissed me on the cheek, and said, "It's a long time since I saw you last. Circumstances being what they are, it isn't surprising that you don't look specially glad to see me."

"We'll go into that presently," I answered. "The police and an ambulance will be here any moment now."

"You're sure the old chap's dead?"

"He looks it. It looks as if the car went right over his chest. You want to stay here tonight, do you?"

Whenever he suddenly came into my life in Allingford he generally wanted at least a room for the night.

"If I may, though not, of course, if it's inconvenient," he said. "I mean, if you're going to be busy with the police and so on."

He was always shy of meeting the police, though he had never, to my knowledge, actually got into their hands.

"Oh, you can stay, but you'd better move your car," I said. "You shouldn't park in front of a person's garage."

"I know, but there were reasons . . . I mean, I didn't think. Don't bother about it now, I'll move it by and by. Ah, here's the ambulance."

The ambulance and a police car arrived almost at the same time. I stood beside Felix by his car, waiting to see if I should be wanted, but as the body of Malcolm Creed was lifted carefully into the ambulance the police seemed to want to disperse the crowd. I saw a tall man having a talk with Mrs. Bulpitt and I saw her gesture at me and the man glance towards me. But he showed no sign of wanting to speak to me, so I thought that Felix and I might as well go into the house. He took a suitcase out of his car, locked it, and followed me in.

My unposted letters were lying by the telephone, but they were only some bills that I had been paying and were not at all urgent. We went into the sitting-room, which was not at all a distinguished room, but I was fond of it. There was too much furniture in it, of too many different periods, but it was comfortable and I thought friendly. If I had ever let Felix get to work on it he would soon have turned it into something far more elegant and perhaps no less friendly, for he was far cleverer than I was at such things; but he would probably have wanted to throw out a number of the things that my mother had collected during her long life, and which had always been there in my childhood as she and I moved from house to house after my father's death in the war.

She had lived longer in Allingford than anywhere else, but she had been one of the people who do not know how to settle anywhere. She had always had good reasons for believing that the grass would be greener in another field. And I appeared to have inherited a certain amount of this from her, for I had never felt that I belonged anywhere in particular, or, if it came to that, to anyone in particular either. I had believed fervently for a short time that Felix and I could build a stable and beautiful life together, beginning very happily in a flat in a fine but dilapidated Georgian house in Little Carberry Street in Bloomsbury, but that dream had not lasted long. A sad thing was that I had believed I could bring some order and security into his erratic life, and had not realized that those were things I was looking for myself.

He moved towards the fireplace where there was a good fire burning, very welcome on this cold, damp November

evening. Lighting a cigarette, he tossed the used match into
the flames. At nearly forty-five he was still very good-looking, though the hair that had looked simply fair in the lamp-
light of the street I could now see had a good deal of grey in
it, while faint lines had fanned out from the corners of his
very bright blue eyes. As always, he was dressed conserva-
tively and well. His suit was dark grey, his shirt was of grey
and white stripes, and his tie was a soft, dark red. He was of
medium height and still slender, and if the boyishness that had
lasted well into his thirties had faded, it had been replaced by
an air of distinction. People nearly always believed that he
was what he chose to say he was, though this varied a good
deal according to the company that he was in.

I had known him to pass himself off as a professor of
theoretical physics and a Fellow of the Royal Society, and as
a man important in the highest reaches of television, and as a
colonel in a distinguished regiment, invalided out of it because of a wound acquired in a field of action never quite
clearly placed. When I married him I believed him to be an
engineer, working for one of the major construction compa-
nies in the country, only to discover when I tried once to get
in touch with him in one of their offices that they had never
heard of him. In fact, I had discovered then that he was
working for a very dubious second-hand car firm, whose
managing director happened to be in gaol for fraud.

"I'm sorry about things," he said. "You say he was a friend
of yours."

He dropped into a chair beside the fireplace and started
looking around for an ashtray, but as I had not smoked for
ten years it happened that there were none in my house. He
reached out towards the fire and knocked some ash into it. He
was a chain-smoker, always certain that lung cancer, heart

disease, and the other horrors of which we have been so well warned in recent times would only happen to other people, just as he always felt sure that the disguises he liked to assume would not be penetrated, or that he would not be caught for the small frauds that he often perpetrated.

"Yes, anyway a neighbour," I said. "He and his wife are both about eighty and tend to lead a very quiet life, but I should think I know them as well as anybody. His wife's in hospital at the moment, having an operation for gallstones. I believe she's coming home tomorrow or the day after and I've a feeling I must go along and see if I can be of any help to her. I suppose the police will have actually broken the news of poor Malcolm's death to her."

"They haven't any family?" Felix asked.

"No," I said.

"Very tough for her."

"Very. Would you like a drink?"

"Very much."

"Sherry?"

"Yes, please. But don't bother about a meal for me. I can go out into the town."

"It's all right, I can concoct something."

"And I needn't stay here, you know. When I came I wasn't expecting to walk into disaster."

"It's all right," I said again. I was finding that actually I was very glad to have him there. After what had happened it would be chilling, perhaps almost frightening, to be alone. Death brushing us with his wings always brings an inward shudder, a shivering sense of cold. I went to the drinks cupboard and poured out sherry for us both.

Sitting down, I said, "What brought you here?"

"I've been in a job not far away," Felix said, "but it's just

come to an end and I was on my way home and as I had to
drive through Allingford anyway, I thought I'd look in."

"The job's come to an end, has it?"

Felix's jobs had a habit of coming to an end.

"If you mean, have I been sacked, or quarrelled with anyone, or been got rid of for just being plain incompetent, then
no," he said with some bitterness in his voice, as if this was
the sort of thing that he expected from me. But I would
never have suspected him of having quarrelled with anyone.
He was a most peaceable, unquarrelsome man. It had been one
of the things that had made the break in our marriage peculiarly difficult. He simply would not quarrel with me. "It's a
seasonal thing," he said. "The place shuts down in November
— There!" The doorbell had just rung. "That'll be the police."

He was right. Two men stood on my doorstep, a sergeant
and a constable. The sergeant introduced himself as Sergeant
George Madden and the constable as James Baker, and said
that they would like to have a few words with me. The
sergeant was the big man whom I had seen talking to Mrs.
Bulpitt. He was tall and heavily built and was probably in his
forties, had pale ginger hair receding from his forehead, and
small, pale blue eyes.

Really there had been no need for him to introduce the
constable. I knew him quite well. His wife, Sandra, had been
my household help for the last year, and Jim Baker, who was
a very handy man, had come in a number of times to change
electric light bulbs that were out of my reach, mend washers
on taps, put up some bookshelves, and do other odd jobs
about the house. The Bakers had a four-year-old daughter
called Louella, and Sandra used to bring her with her when
she came to work. That she could do this was one of the

reasons why she was ready to work for me. She was a slim, elegant young woman, always much more smartly turned out than I was, but intimidatingly efficient. It was one of my fears in life that as soon as Louella was old enough to go to school, I should lose her mother, who would find some far more glamorous kind of work.

Jim did not exactly smile at me, the situation being what it was, when he and the sergeant came into the house, but he and I exchanged glances of recognition. I took the two men into the sitting-room and, introducing Felix to them as a relation of mine (which in its way was not untrue and was much easier than wasting time explaining what the relationship was), I asked them to sit down. They did so, but with that slight stiffness on the edge of their chairs which somehow indicated that they did not mean to stay long.

"Mrs. Freer, I believe it was you who telephoned to the police and for an ambulance," the sergeant said.

I nodded.

"And you were one of the first on the scene, so your neighbour Mrs. Bulpitt said," he went on.

"I suppose so," I said. "There seemed to be a lot of people there all at once. I'm not sure who actually got there first."

"How did that come about?" he asked. "Were you in the street at the time?"

"No, I'd just opened my door to go out and post some letters," I said, "then my telephone rang and I turned back to answer it, leaving the door open. And so I heard a scream and the dog yelping and a noise that I thought was made by brakes being jammed on violently. So I ran out and saw the rear-lights of a car disappearing down the street and Mr. Creed lying in the middle of it. It's true that he's dead, is it, Sergeant?"

"Yes, I'm afraid so. Killed instantaneously. Mrs. Freer, can you tell me, when you first opened your door, did you see anyone on either side of the street? If we can find a witness to the accident, it might be useful."

I closed my eyes for a moment, trying to visualize what I had actually seen in the brief glimpse that I had had outside before the telephone started to ring, but except for the semi-darkness of the evening and the fog I could remember nothing. I shook my head.

"Of course I wasn't thinking about it," I said. "There may have been someone there, but I really didn't notice anything."

"And all you saw of the car when you came back to the door was its rear-lights disappearing?"

"Yes."

"You're sure of that?"

"My impression is it was a big car, but I couldn't tell you the make."

"It was a silver-grey Jaguar," Felix said suddenly. "I'm almost sure it was."

The sergeant turned towards him as if for the first time becoming aware of his presence.

"Then you saw the accident, sir?" he said.

"No," Felix said. "I was just arriving here when I saw a car ahead of me swerve in the road, then drive on at high speed to the end of it and disappear round the corner. I wasn't even sure there'd been an accident till I saw a number of people come running out of their houses and saw that there was someone lying there."

"That's your car at the gate, is it?"

"Yes."

"And you'd come from where?"

"The village of Redgarth. I've been working there for some months."

I wondered what work Felix could possibly have been doing in Redgarth. It was a not very interesting village about fifteen miles from Allingford. It was mostly inhabited by retired people who had taken over what had once been farm labourers' cottages, put in central heating, double glazing, dishwashers, and freezers. If sometimes they thought of moving away into old people's homes or to tax havens, they were liable to be able to sell their cottages for eighty or ninety thousand pounds. But unless Felix had taken up gardening and had been keeping their village spruce for them, I could not think what he could have been doing there.

The sergeant turned back to me. "I understand from Mrs. Bulpitt that Mrs. Creed is in hospital."

"Yes, in St. Mary's," I said. "She had an operation for gallstones, but I think she'll be coming home in a day or two."

"Poor woman," he said. "The news will have to be broken to her this evening, I suppose. My job, probably. Is there anyone else living in her house?"

"I don't think so."

"It's just that naturally we knocked and rang and all that, but there was no answer. So she'll be coming straight home from hospital to an empty house, will she? It seems hard. Can anything be done for her?"

"I'll see what I can do," I said. "Anyway, I'll go to see her tomorrow and perhaps Mrs. Bulpitt will be able to help. She's involved in a lot of good works in the town. I think she's on the committee of a group called Help in Need, or something like that, who send out people to look after disabled people.

Not nurses, you know, but just women who can look after you for a time."

"Good," he said. "Good. And I suppose Mrs. Creed can stay on in hospital till you've got something fixed up for her."

"Well, you know how they are these days," I said. "They boot you out the moment they're sure you aren't going to die on their hands. But I expect Mrs. Bulpitt can arrange something."

He turned his head sharply to look at Felix once more.

"Did you see anything of who was driving the car?" he asked.

"No," Felix said. "That is—no."

I felt that he had almost told the sergeant something that might be of importance, but had restrained himself. But even if he had said what had first come into his mind it might not have been the truth. He might for a moment have felt tempted to give a vivid description of a red-haired man with dark glasses and a sinister air who had come striding along the pavement, leapt into a stationary car, and driven off. But if he had done that he would of course have had to account for the presence of the stationary car and how he had been able to discern how sinister the man had looked, yet had not been able to say more about the accident.

"And you saw nothing of the driver, Mrs. Freer?" the sergeant said. "Not even if it was a man or a woman?"

"I think I hardly looked at the car," I said. "It was halfway down the street already before I got out, and then I only looked at poor Mr. Creed."

"Yes, naturally. Well, thank you for your help."

He stood up and so did Jim Baker. I saw them to the door. As they went, Jim made a little gesture to me, expressing the fact that although this was an official visit, of course we were friends. Returning to my neglected glass of sherry, I wished that I had chosen something stronger. Although I could see that my hands were steady, I felt as if inwardly my very skeleton was shaking.

"Felix, what's this about your working in Redgarth?" I asked as I sat down. "What is there to do there?"

He tossed his cigarette into the fire and lit another.

"I've been a guide at Redgarth House," he answered. "Is there anything peculiar about that?"

I thought that there was a good deal that was peculiar, yet it was not impossible. Redgarth House was a Palladian mansion, very handsome, which stood in a fine park full of great old chestnut trees and which was about two miles from the village. It belonged now, I had heard, to an Arab who besides being immensely rich was a passionate collector of artwork of all descriptions, and who had lately thrown his house open to the public on certain days of the week. On those days, of course, a guide would be needed, or perhaps more than one, to show the public round, and Felix might somehow have landed a job there for himself.

"But you don't know anything about pictures and furniture and old silver and so on," I said. "How could you guide anyone round?"

"Oh, you soon learn the routine," he answered. "There are pamphlets that tell you all you need to know, and of course you can elaborate on them a bit, and most people who come round know so little that you could make it up as you go along. It's true you occasionally run into an expert and then you have to take a bit more trouble with your act. My line is generally to behave apologetically, implying that though I happen to be one of the family, who's just standing in for the

professional for the day, I really don't know much about my
own ancestors. Then I act as if I couldn't be more sorry that I
can't ask them to stay for tea and meet my sisters, but I must
get on with my work."

"What nonsense, Felix," I said. "No one could take you
for an Arab. And an Arab wouldn't dream of inviting some
complete strangers to meet his sisters."

"Oh, I don't pretend I'm related to the Arab. I have to be
more subtle than that. I imply, if I'm driven to it, that I'm
part of the family who used to own the house but who are so
poverty-stricken that they were compelled to sell it to a mil-
lionaire from Saudi Arabia, and that I think myself lucky to
be able to hang around a bit as I love it so much. Of course,
some of them don't believe me for a moment, but they're too
polite to say so openly. It's extraordinary how polite people
are. I know I'd be polite myself in the same circumstances,
whatever I said about it later."

"But the job's come to an end now?"

"Yes, the tourist season's over. It'll begin again at Easter
next year."

"And will you go back to it?"

"I might unless something more interesting turns up in the
interval."

"And you've been living in Redgarth all this summer, so
near to Allingford, yet you didn't think of coming to see
me."

He looked embarrassed. "Well, you know how it is, Virginia. If I do turn up suddenly I'm never certain that you're
in the least pleased to see me, and that's humiliating. I don't
want to force myself on you when you don't want me
around. I thought I'd risk it this evening as I'd got to drive

through Allingford anyway, but I was quite prepared to be thrown out."

"I don't believe I've ever actually thrown you out."

This was true. When he and I had separated I had, so to speak, thrown myself out of the flat in Little Carberry Street, where I had known first such happiness, then such agonies of indecision, and finally a kind of bleak despair about which there had been a kind of acceptance, which in its way had been healing. But whenever Felix had appeared in Ellsworthy Street, once I had settled there, I had always, after a fashion, made him welcome.

"No," he agreed, "you've never actually spat in my face. And that reminds me . . ."

He started feeling in his pockets and after a moment brought out something wrapped in tissue paper. Undoing the wrapping, he showed me a pair of ear-rings, round studs which might have been gold, each of which had a charming little design of a rose in the centre and an edging of seed pearls.

"I thought I shouldn't come empty-handed," he said, "and I thought you might like them."

I did; that was the trouble, for I thought it most unlikely that Felix, however he had obtained them, had simply paid for them. He was a skilled and dedicated shop-lifter, and I thought it was probable that these pretty ear-rings had been quietly slipped into his pocket while their owner, whether in some antique shop in Redgarth or some jeweller in Allingford, had been busy showing him things which he had not the least intention of buying.

He had never been able to think of shop-lifting as a crime. He had always regarded it more as a kind of sport and nearly always made presents of his plunder to his friends. When I

had first known him I had been immensely touched by his
generosity to me. It was only after I had received a number of
delightful gifts from him that I happened to notice him slip-
ping a very expensive lipstick into his pocket, which he had
later presented to me, and I realized that he had paid for none
of the things that he had given me. Going out shopping with
him after that was a nightmare, because I was certain that one
day he was bound to be caught. But surprisingly, so far this
had never happened to him.

"Where did you nick them?" I asked. But I could not resist
putting the ear-rings on and looking at myself in the mirror
over the fireplace.

"I didn't nick them, I bought them," he said indignantly.
"If I'd remembered what you're like I'd have brought the
receipt along with me."

He always treated my reluctance to be a receiver of stolen
property as if it was a kind of eccentricity.

"They didn't come from Redgarth House?" I said. My
resistance to accepting the gift crumbled when I saw how nice
I thought I looked, wearing the ear-rings.

"Good God, no!" he exclaimed and sounded genuinely
shocked. "I was in a position of trust, wasn't I? Besides, I
believe old Abou Ben Adhem, may his tribe increase, knows
absolutely everything, down to the last teaspoon, that he's got
in that mansion."

"And charming as these are, I don't suppose they're in his
class. Are they really gold?"

"I shouldn't think so. I couldn't have afforded them if they
were. But you quite like them, do you?"

"Very much. Thank you, Felix. It was nice of you not to
come empty-handed."

He smiled for the first time since he had arrived. He had a

warm, attractive smile which still affected me more than I altogether wanted.

"Then what shall we have to eat?" he asked. "Would you like to go out?"

"I don't think we ought to, in case the police want me again," I said. "I'll get something out of the freezer. And I've got some cheese and some fruit and even a bottle of wine which you might open for me."

"And I can stay the night?"

"Let's go and make your bed now, then we can settle down peacefully with our drinks."

Together we made up the bed in my small spare bedroom, after I had taken a packet of pasta with seafood out of my freezer and put it to warm in my oven. Then I added some coal to the fire in the sitting-room, poked it up into flames, after which we sat down again with our second drinks.

We did not talk much. I was thinking of the old man whose body I had seen taken away in the ambulance, not to any hospital, I supposed, but to a mortuary. He had been in the RAF, I believed, during the war, and come through it unscathed, then he and his wife had tried farming in Kenya and avoided being murdered there by the Mau Mau, and then at last, out walking his dog one evening in Ellsworthy Street, he had been knocked down and killed by some casually ruthless or merely incompetent driver. But thinking about that reminded me of something that Felix had said while we were still out in the road.

"Felix, you parked your car right in front of my garage," I said. "You began to say there were reasons why you'd done it, then you stopped yourself. Just what were the reasons?"

"Oh well . . ." he said vaguely, reaching for another of his eternal cigarettes. "It was nothing really. Just carelessness."

"No," I said. "You had a reason."

He frowned as he lit the cigarette. He was trying to make up his mind whether or not to tell me the truth about why he had done it.

"The fact is, with so many cars parked along the street, I turned automatically into the first empty space I saw," he said.

"But if you'd gone only a few yards farther on, you'd have left my gate clear and could have parked in front of the house. There was nothing there— Oh no, I see!" I exclaimed. "There *was* something there. You mean that car, the silver-grey Jaguar, was parked there."

He fingered the inside of his collar uneasily.

"I'm not sure. Perhaps it wasn't actually parked there, or anyway, only for a moment," he said. "I really don't know. Everything happened so quickly."

"Not as quickly as all that. You took your time, parking your car, and then you only stood beside it, looking on, while the rest of us rushed up to where Mr. Creed was lying."

"Yes," he said. "Yes, that's quite true."

"So what really happened?"

"Well, this bloody car swerved out and I had to jam on my brakes, and then there I was in front of your garage, so I stayed there. I'll go out and move it now, if you like."

"Wait a moment," I said. "When I opened my door to go out and post my letters there wasn't any silver-grey Jaguar in front of my house."

"There wasn't?" He sounded as if he did not altogether believe me. "You're sure?"

"Look, tell me exactly what you saw," I said.

He blew out a cloud of smoke and watched it disperse before he answered. Then he spoke unwillingly.

"I'll tell you what I saw, but I may be wrong about some of it. This car was in front of your house and someone was staggering along the pavement to it and got in and drove off. Dead drunk, I thought. And there was your door standing open and light streaming out, so I took for granted he'd come out of your house."

"I haven't been entertaining any drunks lately."

"Then perhaps I was wrong, as I said, and the car was actually parked in front of your neighbour's house and only began to move towards me as I drove up. But the moment this character I saw was inside it, the thing shot forwards and swerved out into the road, and the next thing I heard was a scream and the dog yelping and all that."

It was not impossible. Mrs. Bulpitt's house and mine were semi-detached, each with a garage on its free side. If a car had been parked in front of Mrs. Bulpitt's house when I first opened my door I should probably not have noticed it, and if the car had moved off swiftly as I turned back into the house to answer the telephone, I should not have seen it. And if Felix by then had been parked to the side of my house, in front of my garage, I might not have noticed that either, for at that stage all that I was thinking about was the still, dark form in the road.

But Mrs. Bulpitt had seemed even angrier than the rest of us at the car not stopping, and had shown no sign of guessing to whom it might have belonged. Also I found it difficult to imagine her entertaining drunks.

"What sort of person is this neighbour of yours?" Felix asked.

"I don't know her awfully well," I said. "She's been living

next door for about two years and we have coffee together quite often and gossip, but I don't know a great deal about her. We still call each other Mrs. Bulpitt and Mrs. Freer. I know that the moment she arrived in Allingford she got involved in all the local good works. I think she'd been secretary of some charity or other in London before she retired. But I don't know who Mr. Bulpitt was, or if she's got any family, or how well off she is. She's a domineering sort of person with a rather explosive temper, and she's generally got some complaint to make about the behaviour of someone on one of her committees, but I think she's kind in her way . . ." I paused. An odd thought had just struck me.

"Well?" Felix said.

"I just wondered if it was possible, if you really saw a drunk come staggering out of her house, if he was one of her hard cases whom she was trying to help. I can't imagine that the occasion can have been simply social."

"Hard cases who drive off in Jaguars?" Felix asked sceptically.

"Well, suppose he was an alcoholic, or on drugs or something. Alcoholics can be quite wealthy. Most of them have to be."

"Actually I didn't see him come out of her house, you know," he said. "I only saw him on the pavement."

"But you're sure it was a man, are you? It couldn't have been a woman?"

"I think it was a man. But since you ask me, I'm not dead certain. It's often difficult to tell the difference nowadays."

I nodded. Both sexes wear trousers, and a woman with short hair or a man with long could easily be wrongly identified.

I finished my sherry and got up to go and attend to the

dish in the oven. But before I went there was one more thing
that I wanted to ask.

"Felix, why didn't you tell any of this, I mean about the
man or woman on the pavement, and seeing the car drive off
and so on, to the police? It's just the kind of thing they want
to know."

"Yes, well, perhaps I should have, but you see . . ." He
gave another smile, a rather sad one this time. "We hadn't
talked it over and I didn't want to risk getting you into
trouble. Of course I believe you when you say that drunk
didn't come out of your house and that the car wasn't parked
in front of it, but how was I to be sure they'd believe you
too. As a matter of fact, I doubt if they would for a moment."

TWO

THE POLICE did not come back that evening. Felix opened a bottle of wine and we sat down to a very silent meal in the kitchen. I was thinking of what I should have to do next day, go to St. Mary's Hospital and see if I could help Julia Creed. My sympathy had shifted quickly, as I believe is usually the case, from Malcolm, by now lying quietly dead in a mortuary, to Julia who had to face the fact of her bereavement. It is probably the survivor who suffers most. The Creeds had been a very affectionate couple, very dependent on one another, and Julia, even though all had gone well with her operation, would be a sick woman for some time after she came home. I would have to see what I could do for her.

I went to see her at eleven o'clock next day, the hour at which visitors were admitted to the hospital. Felix, as his custom had always been, had brought me a cup of tea in bed, then I had gone downstairs, made coffee and toast for our breakfast, then got dressed and greeted Sandra Baker, who came in every morning to clean my house. She was slim and very pretty with short blonde hair, big grey eyes, and a smooth, pale complexion. As usual, she was smartly dressed in well-cut black slacks and a scarlet sweater, with a number of gold chains round her neck. The first thing that she did on arriving was to put on rubber gloves, but she never descended to wearing an apron or overall. She had Louella with her, a large, burly, thoughtful child who followed her mother round from room to room without ever making much attempt to get into conversation with me.

"Jim told me what happened here last night," Sandra said to me as she began cleaning out the grate in the sitting-room, before laying a new fire there. "Terrible, isn't it. I mean, knocking the poor old fellow down and then just driving on. Jim says he doesn't think they'll ever find who did it, though they've been questioning all the people along the road in case someone saw something. Queer, isn't it, you can have two or three hundred people killed in an aeroplane crash and it's splashed all over television, but you can have as many as that killed on the roads and you don't hear a word about it. If they was one day to say a day had gone by without anybody being killed, you'd think that would really be news, but it seems it isn't."

"Sandra, I don't suppose you've any spare time yourself at the moment," I said, "but do you happen to know of anyone who might like to do a job for Mrs. Creed? Just for a little while. She'll be coming out of hospital in a day or two and she'll be very weak. I want to find someone who could go in and look after her at least for a short time."

She swept up the grate and crumpled a newspaper to lay in it. She looked sympathetic.

"You know how it is, Mrs. Freer, I'll go in gladly to do a bit of cleaning, if that will be any help, but I've Louella to look after and I couldn't actually go to stay in the house, which is what Mrs. Creed will really want, isn't it? And offhand I can't think of anyone who's free, but I'll ask around."

"Thank you," I said. "I think I'll ask Mrs. Bulpitt if she knows of anyone. I'm going to the hospital now."

I was not looking forward to it. I put Sandra's money out on the kitchen table, then I went looking for Felix, whom I found sitting on the edge of his bed, reading my copy of *The Times* in the little spare bedroom. What struck me first as I went into the room was that the bed had been neatly made. It had not been taken to pieces with the sheets folded up, which was what he would have done, being a very neat man, if the use of the bed was over. It looked as if he was thinking of staying on for at least another night.

"Are you staying on then?" I asked.

"I haven't really thought about it yet," he said. "Do you want me to leave?"

"Not particularly."

"And you're going to the hospital now?"

"Yes."

"Then let's talk about it when you get back."

"So anyway you'll be here for lunch."

"If you don't mind."

"I've nothing much in the house but we could go the Red Lion and have some fish and chips," I said.

The Red Lion was a pub at the far end of Ellsworthy Street.

"That sounds fine," he said.

I left him, went out to the garage, and got my car out. Felix had already moved his out of the way.

Setting off to drive to St. Mary's Hospital, I felt somewhat apprehensive and deeply depressed at the thought of having to cope with someone else's grief. Julia Creed was not in bed when I arrived. She was in a chair beside her bed in a ward that contained three other people, and was wearing a pretty pale blue dressing-gown and had her white hair neatly combed. She was slumped in the chair, her face vacant and her brown eyes dull and empty. She was a small woman, rather plump, with a round face which, in spite of being deeply wrinkled, was normally pink and full of life, but which this morning was so expressionless as to be almost like a mask.

One of the nurses saw that I was going to speak to her and came up to me and whispered in my ear.

"Poor dear, she doesn't know what's hit her. It's fearful, isn't it? She'd been making such a good recovery too. The police were in here yesterday evening and broke the news to her about her husband and she didn't seem to take it in at first. She seemed almost cheerful. Then we gave her sleeping-pills, of course, and she had a good night, but this morning she's just like you see her. She doesn't seem to know what's going on. But she insisted on getting up, although the doctor said she should stay in bed."

"When is she supposed to be coming home?" I asked.

"Tomorrow, if she's up to it. That's when she was supposed to be going, but things being as they are, of course we won't turn her out. Only she seems to want to go as soon as she can."

"Well, thanks," I said, and the nurse left me.

I went up to Julia, leant over her, and kissed her on the cheek. For a moment she seemed to shrink from me, then looked me long and full in the face and murmured, "Oh, it's you, Virginia."

"I came to see if there's anything I can do to help," I said.

"That's nice of you," she said in the same soft, murmuring

voice, so that I was only just able to hear her. "I'm going home tomorrow, you know."

"So the nurse just told me."

"The nurses here are all very nice. They've been very good to me."

"I'm glad to hear that. But do you think you really ought to come home tomorrow? Wouldn't it be better to stay on here for at least another day or two?"

"Oh dear, they wouldn't like that," she said. "I'm really quite well, you see, and of course they need the bed as soon as they can have it for other emergencies."

"But the nurse said you could stay on," I said. "She seemed to think it would be best."

"But I think I ought to go home," she said. "I want to go home. There'll be so much to arrange, you know. His funeral first. He wanted to be cremated, so I must see to that. I don't know what I'll do with the ashes. What does one do? I wouldn't want to keep them just in the house. Then I'll have to see our lawyer. And there's Jinks, of course."

"Who's Jinks?" I asked.

"Our dog. Our dear old dog."

I had completely forgotten about the dog. That seemed very callous now.

"Don't worry about him," I said. "I think one of the women from down the street is looking after him."

She gave me a doubtful look. "Is that true? The police said nothing about him, except that he hadn't—hadn't been killed. Someone's really looking after him, are they? How kind people can be. But you aren't just saying that to reassure me?"

"No, honestly I think someone picked him up and carried him home. And I'm sure you aren't fit to cope with all the other things. You can't stay in that house alone. If I can, I'll get someone to go in to look after you, or at least I'll go in myself till you're over the worst. But really I'd stay here for the present."

She shook her head with a gentle stubbornness, and it occurred to me I had noticed this quality in her before, but had never come up against it myself.

"No dear, I'm going home tomorrow," she said in the same whispering voice as before, as if she could not bear the thought that any of the other patients in the ward might overhear her. "It's all arranged. I've a taxi coming for me at twelve o'clock and I'll be perfectly well able to look after myself. It's very sweet of you to offer, but I shan't need any help."

This was so obviously untrue that I did not trouble to argue with her. But her determination made it urgent that help should be arranged at once. I could stay with her, at least in the evenings, for a day or two, but I had my job to think about and it would be more than a day or two before she would be able to look after herself. I supposed that if Malcolm had been there he would have managed to look after her. That was probably what they had planned. But the house without him, cold, silent, and desolate, was not the right place to receive a woman still weakened by serious illness.

"Well, we'll see what we can do," I said, making up my mind as I said it to call on Mrs. Bulpitt on my way home.

After that we chatted for a little while, mostly about the hospital, about the young surgeon from Hong Kong who had operated on her, the strange effects that various drugs had had on her, and all the other things that dominate the mind of a person who has suddenly had to endure unaccustomed illness. But from time to time Julia's face became completely blank and she seemed to lose the thread of what she had been say-

ing; times, I thought, when something which was still really
incomprehensible to her had forced its way into her understanding. I did not stay long. I went back to my car and
drove to Ellsworthy Street, put the car into my garage, then
walked back to Mrs. Bulpitt's door.

She answered my ring and somehow gave me the impression, as she greeted me, that she had been expecting me. I
understood why this was when she took me into her sitting-
room, for I found Felix there. They had been drinking coffee
together. There were cups and a coffee-pot on a table.

"You'll have some coffee," she said. "Wait a moment, I'll
get a cup."

She shot out of the room. Her movements always had a
kind of aggressive rapidity about them. Her little withered
face generally had an expression that suggested she was ready
to pick a quarrel with anyone who would give her a chance
to do so. But her smile was friendly, and though we had
never become intimate we had never come near to a quarrel.
She was wearing a worn and rather soiled purple cardigan
and a drooping grey skirt.

When she left the room I looked at Felix with raised
eyebrows, implying the question of what he was doing there.

He answered in a whisper, "I went out for a stroll. She
pounced out and nabbed me."

"Why?"

"Curiosity about what I was doing here, I think."

"Did you tell her who you are?"

"Oh yes, everything's out in the open."

Mrs. Bulpitt came charging back. She had a cup and saucer
with her, asked me if I wanted my coffee black or white,
poured it out, and flung herself down in a chair.

"Your husband's been telling me you'd gone to the hospital

to see poor Julia," she said. "I was hoping you'd come in and tell me how she is. He's also been telling me about his extraordinary adventures this summer. Whoever would think anything like that could happen in a quiet little place like Redgarth. Spies, terrorists, kidnapping—but they freed the poor unhappy girl, I was glad to hear, though God knows what ransom they paid. Of course he says it will be kept out of the newspapers. All very confidential. And with his job there done he can go back to his work in London. It's really interesting to meet someone who's involved in Intelligence work, you know. I don't think I ever have before."

She had not done so yet, though I thought it would be complicated to enlighten her. I did think that it was a little strange that she should apparently have been so ready to believe that someone engaged in Intelligence work should have confided in her so fully at a first meeting, but then I noticed what I thought was an ironic glint in her eyes and wondered if she knew quite well that Felix had merely been entertaining himself, and he hoped her, with some of his fantasies.

I met his gaze. It was bland and unrevealing. He knew that I was unlikely to go so far as to tell her there and then what a liar he was.

"I only played a very small part in it all," he said modestly. "Really nothing to speak of."

"And I've been thinking of the tragic accident here last night as a kind of adventure," she said. "Isn't that dreadful? But of course it was exciting in its horrible way. Most of us lead very drab lives and when something as atrocious as that accident happens, with the horrible driver just going straight on, it creates a sort of morbid excitement, doesn't it? I know we'll go on talking about it for weeks. I hardly slept at all last night, I was so tense with shock. You were lucky to have Mr. Freer with you."

I knew that I had been. But it surprised me in a way to hear Mrs. Bulpitt call her existence drab. With all her committees, her work on appeals for charities, and her occasional public speaking on their behalf, which was reported at length in the local press, she always seemed very busily employed in a way which I should have thought a woman of her stamp would find tolerably colourful.

It was true that her surroundings were very drab. When she had first moved into the house she had had nothing redecorated. She had taken over carpets and curtains from the previous owners and still had not replaced them, even though everything had already been faded when she took the things over. Her furniture was curiously on the pretentious side, yet was somehow shabby and not very clean. She had some grubby plastic roses in a vase on the mantelpiece which had been there for as long as I had known her. My impression of her was that she was a relatively poor woman who had seen much better days, perhaps when the husband of whom I had never heard her speak had still been alive, and that her good works were to a considerable extent a way of entertaining herself without their costing her anything significant.

"It's rather worrying," I said as I sat down with my coffee, "Julia insists on coming home tomorrow and she simply isn't fit to look after herself. That's partly why I came round. I thought perhaps you might know of someone who could move in to look after her for a little while. Doesn't that group you belong to, Help in Need, supply people for that sort of thing?"

She considered my question, sipping her coffee.

"Yes, if there's someone available," she said. "I'll see what I can do. Of course, I'd offer to help myself, but you know how busy I am. I ought to be able to arrange something, though. She's coming home tomorrow, you said. So I'd better get busy as soon as I can. How is she?"

"Stunned, I think," I said. "I don't think she'll really take in what's happened till she gets home. I believe she's made a quite good recovery from the operation, but when she gets home the thing will really hit her."

"Poor dear," she said. "They were so devoted to one another, weren't they? I used to envy them, you know, having each other, not having a lonely old age before them. But she's a little old to start developing new interests now, isn't she? It would be such a help if she could. I wonder if she's got any family anywhere. I never knew what brought them to Allingford."

"What brought you to Allingford?" Felix asked. "In a way it seems a strange place to settle unless you've connections here."

"Well, you see, I was born here," she said, "and stayed here till I was over twenty. I had a very happy childhood. And so when I retired from my job in London I suddenly took it into my head to return here. Perhaps it was a mistake. People say one shouldn't go back to places where one's been happy, it's always a disappointment. But on the whole it's worked pretty well. I've some nice friends, your wife among them, and of course some very interesting activities. I'm not really a person who's dependent on her surroundings. I believe I could be content almost anywhere."

"And you think you can find someone to help Julia," I said, sticking to the point.

"Probably, yes," she said. "In any case, I'll let you know later today. I'm sure we'll be able to arrange something."

"Julia was worried about her dog," I said. "Do you know what's happened to him?"

"I think Mrs. Greenfield's looking after him."

Mrs. Greenfield was a woman who lived a little way down the road and was usually to be seen, mornings and evenings, walking a weary-looking castrated Labrador, an uppish little poodle, and an Airedale puppy along the street towards the open common at one end of it. I remembered that it was she who had gathered the Creeds' dog into her arms after the accident, making sure that it had not been seriously hurt.

"That dog could tell us what really happened, if only he could speak," Mrs. Bulpitt went on.

"You didn't see anything yourself?" Felix asked.

She shook her head. "I just heard poor old Malcolm cry out and the dog making a noise, and so I came running out. The car was gone by then."

"And yet, d'you know, its seems likely it may have been parked in front of your house?" he said.

She made a queer little convulsive gesture as she sat in her chair, and did not look up to meet his eyes, but went on thoughtfully looking into her coffee.

"How strange," she said. "What makes you think that?"

"You see, I arrived just as the accident happened," he said, "and I saw a car pull away from the kerb here and do a wild swerve in the street. It might have come from farther on, of course, except that cars were parked pretty solid most of the way along. There was just this empty space in front of your house and Virginia's."

"If the car swerved, it was to avoid hitting Malcolm, I suppose."

"It could have been."

"That's what I said at first, isn't it?" she said, turning to

look at me. "I said perhaps the driver couldn't help it if
Malcolm walked out right in front of him. It was the driving
on without stopping that's so shocking. But it's just possible,
isn't it, that he didn't realize what he'd done? I wonder if that
could be the explanation."

"Of course you don't know anything about who it was,"
Felix said.

Her fierce look appeared on her face.

"Certainly not. I was in the kitchen at the time. The window overlooks the garden at the back. In any case, I wasn't
looking out. I was cooking myself a spinach flan. I'm particularly partial to spinach flan. And even though I live by myself
and have no one else to cook for, I do quite a lot of cooking.
I think one should feed oneself properly, even if one's alone.
That flan is really excellent." She looked back at me. "I'll
give you the recipe if you like."

I thanked her, though I am not one of the people who can
work up much enthusiasm about cooking for only myself. I
buy a lot from Marks and Spencer. Felix and I left soon after
that.

As we were walking towards my gate he said, "Of course
she did see the driver."

"Why d'you think so?" I said.

"She talked too much about not seeing it. And she was
nervous when I said the car could have been parked in front
of her house."

"I think the way you suddenly took to questioning her
might have made anyone nervous."

We turned in at my gate, I unlocked my front door, and
we went in. Sandra and Louella had gone by then and the
house had the peculiarly neat, tidy look it always had when
Sandra has just been there. I poured out sherry for us both.

"Is that woman really as poor as she appears?" he asked as I put a match to the fire that Sandra had laid in the sitting-room grate.

"I don't know," I said. "It isn't the sort of thing one asks people, is it? Actually she's talked about how difficult it is to make ends meet with inflation and all, but I don't know what that means. We've all got different standards about our poverty or affluence. For instance, I generally speaking feel I'm pretty well off, having gone through a period of genuine poverty when I was young, but I expect to a good many people even now I may seem near to the poverty line."

He shook his head. "This house is comfortable and well cared for and you're always nicely turned out, if not in the height of fashion, and anyone can see you've got as much as you want. But that house next door is pretty squalid and what she was wearing was practically sordid. So is she as poor as all that, or is she a miser, or has she a heart of gold and gives most of what she has to charity?"

"I just don't know," I said.

"And you don't know anything about the late—I presume the late—Mr. Bulpitt?"

"Not a thing."

"I somehow don't believe in the heart of gold," he said.

It was a matter to which I had never given any thought. I had taken Mrs. Bulpitt as just what she appeared to be, and had never thought of her as in any way mysterious. I was not inclined to do so now. Felix had a passion for finding mysteries where there were none.

"Why did you tell her all that stuff about some poor character being kidnapped at Redgarth?" I asked.

"We had to talk about something, hadn't we?" he said. "I was just strolling past, thinking of going to the shops to pick up something for lunch so that we didn't have to go out to the Red Lion, when she pounced out on me and hauled me in to have coffee. I think she was just curious about who you had staying with you. So I had to think of something to say. By the way, what are we going to do about lunch?"

"If you don't want to go out I can give you a ham sandwich," I said. "But why couldn't you tell her the truth instead of making up a yarn like that? There must be quite a lot of interesting things to say about a place like Redgarth House. Of course she didn't believe you."

"Oh, I think she did."

Felix always believed that his lies were far more convincing than the truth could ever be. What happened to him when he was a child to bring this about I did not know, though I was fairly sure, piecing together the odds and ends that he had told me from time to time, that his father had been a stupid bully of a man who tended to be brutal when he was told the simple truth about some misdemeanour, but could easily be hoodwinked by some colourful fantasy. I believed that he had been in the army, and though Felix was inclined to let it be thought that he had been a colonel, I was fairly convinced that he had been a sergeant. Also I was doubtful of Felix's claim to have been at a public school, albeit a minor one, and thought that at best it had been the local grammar school.

He went on, "If she's really the kind of person she appears to be, it seems a little strange that she should be visited by the kind of person who runs a Jaguar. She doesn't seem to be in the Jaguar class."

"Oh, I don't know about that," I said. "As I said before, it might have been a visit from one of her hard cases. If you're right that whoever it was was drunk, he might have descended on her in the hope of a little help. But if he wasn't drunk at all but perhaps was staggering a bit because he'd got a wooden leg or something like that, then why shouldn't he be someone who's quite wealthy who's involved with her in her charitable activities?"

"If that was so, why the insistence that she didn't know the car was in front of her house and all that nonsense about the spinach flan? If he was really one of her hard cases, perhaps she had to be confidential about his visit, though it's going a bit far to try to protect a drunk driver who runs over someone and doesn't stop. That's a very serious offence. I see she might want to protect someone whose money's important in some charity affair. She might be desperate to avoid a scandal. But even if that's so I find something curious about the whole affair."

To be honest, so did I, now that he had pointed it out to me, but I did not feel like being dragged into a highly speculative discussion of what had happened the evening before, the facts of which were not really known to me. Felix might be telling the truth about what he had seen, or he might at least have embroidered on it. That he did sometimes tell the truth and could be a very observant and reliable witness could make conversation with him confusing.

My mind went to the ham sandwiches that I was intending to make.

"By the way, how long are you thinking of staying?" I asked.

"Why, d'you want me to leave?" he said. "I can pack up and go right now, if that's what you want."

"No, of course not, I was only thinking of the food I've got in the house," I said. "I'd better go out and do some shopping after lunch. Not just for ourselves. I think I'd better get some supplies in for Julia. If she's really coming home tomorrow to an empty house it may help if there's plenty of food in the fridge."

"Do you think your friend next door will really find someone to help her?"

He managed to give the phrase "your friend" a curiously offensive sound. He seemed to have taken a pronounced dislike to Mrs. Bulpitt, though to do such a thing was very unusual with him. He was normally tolerant of nearly everybody if they only showed signs of feeling some liking for him, and since Mrs. Bulpitt had carried him off into her house to give him coffee, and when I joined them they had appeared to be on reasonably friendly terms, I could not see why he should have any particularly hostile feeling towards her. Perhaps it was simply that he knew quite well that she had not believed his story of the kidnapping at Redgarth House.

As it happened, Mrs. Bulpitt telephoned only a short time after Felix and I had eaten our sandwiches, just as we were preparing to go out and do the shopping that I had in mind.

"It's all right, I'm delighted to tell you," she said. "I've found someone to help Julia. She can move in tomorrow morning. A nice girl called Sue Lockett. A bit young, perhaps, only twenty-five or so, but very practical, and she's been working for Help in Need for the last year. We've had very good reports of her."

"That's splendid news," I said. "She understands the situation, does she? I mean, that she'll be looking after someone who's not only just out of hospital, but has suffered a terrible emotional shock."

"I explained everything," Mrs. Bulpitt said. "But tell me, talking of that emotional shock, you aren't implying, are you, that poor Julia may be on the edge of—well, call it a mental breakdown? That's the polite word for it. You didn't say anything of the sort this morning. I'm not sure if Sue would be capable of dealing with anything like that."

"No, I don't think there's really any risk of that kind," I said, "and I suppose, if the girl does feel she's getting out of her depth, she can go to you about it."

"Oh, of course. I'll do anything I can to help. But Help in Need doesn't normally take on mental cases. They need very specially trained people for that, and Sue's just a nice girl who got married too young, broke up with her husband, and got stranded in Allingford when he left her. I believe he was a house agent, or something like that. And she'd no training of any kind, so the job we were able to offer her was just what she wanted. She isn't one of the brightest people in the world, you know. She failed to get the degree she'd been working for in Bristol. But she's kind and she's got plenty of common sense."

"It sounds ideal," I said. "It's good of you to have fixed it."

"It's what I'm here for," she stated.

After that, Felix and I set out. It was a Saturday, so the shopping could not be put off. There was a supermarket only a little way from where Ellsworthy Street joined the main road, and I bought bread and butter there, and milk and eggs and some tinned soup and some slices of quiche and a cold chicken and other odds and ends which I thought might make it easy for the new help to dish up a meal for Julia soon after arriving. I did not take the things straight to the Creeds' house because first I had to get the key to it. I had one which hung on a hook in my kitchen. The Creeds had always left a key to their house with me, because both of them had had a nervous fear that one day they were going to lock themselves out, and they had liked the feeling that if this happened I would be able to let them in. It had never actually happened all the time that I had had the key, though once or twice when they had gone away for the regular Christmas holiday, which they spent in Bournemouth, they had asked me to go into the house occasionally and check that there had been no break-in, no flood from burst pipes or fire breaking out. I had conscientiously done this, but had never encountered trouble.

I would have taken my purchases straight over to the Creeds' house after Felix and I reached home, but only a few minutes after we did so and before I sorted out what I had bought for ourselves from what I intended for Julia, my telephone rang.

I picked it up and recited my number.

"Mrs. Freer?" a woman's voice said. "This is Maureen Greenfield. It's about the dog."

"Oh, Jinks," I said.

"Jinks—is that his name?" she said. "I haven't known what to call the poor thing. Mrs. Freer, what shall I do with him? I've been looking after him. Someone had to, of course, but it's a bit difficult because Dickie doesn't like him."

"Dickie—is that your husband?" I asked.

She gave a little titter. "Oh dear, no. My husband's name is Oscar, and he loves every kind of animal, even things like snakes and lizards. You must come in one day and see our collection. Dickie's our poodle and he's really very fierce although he's so small, and he won't put up with an intruder. Old Jake doesn't mind Jinks. Jake's our Labrador and he was doctored, you know, and that makes them much less aggressive than if they're normal, and Peg doesn't mind him, that's our Airedale, because she's only a puppy and anyway she's a bitch, so she isn't too quarrelsome. But Dickie had a fight with poor Jinks this morning and nearly tore one of his ears off. I had to take him to the vet to have it stitched on again. I'm so worried, Mrs. Freer. What do you think I ought to do?"

I had a feeling that I knew the answer to that, though I was reluctant to give it. I like dogs but I have never wanted to keep one in a town, where the poor thing could hardly be allowed out of the house except on a lead. Once in my childhood my mother and I had lived in the country for a time, and we had had a very lively and intelligent mongrel who roamed the countryside at will, sometimes disappearing for as long as a week-end, then coming home again with a very satisfied look on his face, and while he was gone it had never occurred to us to worry about him. That was the right sort of life for a dog, I felt, not what he could be given in Ellsworthy Street.

"Well, if it's really difficult for you," I said, "I'll look after him till Mrs. Creed gets home, then she can decide what's to be done about him."

"Would you really do that?" Mrs. Greenfield asked eagerly. "It would be such a help. Of course Oscar and I love him. I couldn't bear to think of him being neglected. But you do see my difficulty, don't you? Dickie's rather used to running things here."

"You'll have to instruct me about feeding him and so on," I said. "I don't know anything about looking after dogs."

"Oh, I'll bring along some tins of dog-food and biscuits and tell you what to do," she said. "But you go out to work, don't you? I suppose it would be all right to leave him shut up alone in the house while you're out. I mean, naturally he's been house-trained, but he might get rather frightened, feeling he'd been abandoned."

"It's all right," I said. "I've got a guest here who can look after him when I have to go out."

Felix in his way was excellently house-trained too. He would take the dog for his necessary walks, would feed him and keep him company. It meant, of course, that he would have to stay on in Allingford perhaps for a few days, but I had an idea that he was intending to do this anyway and I did not see why he should not earn his keep.

I explained this to him when my conversation with Mrs. Greenfield was finished and he replied that he was glad if he could be of use. It resulted, however, in my having to wait for Mrs. Greenfield to arrive with Jinks, so it was some time before I could go over to the Creeds' house to deliver the supplies that I had bought. By the time she had come and gone, leaving Jinks with us, Felix and I were beginning to feel that we would like a cup of tea, and so when I went across the road with my basket it was dusk.

It also felt very cold, and when I let myself into the house the first thing I thought of was that I ought to turn up the thermostat in the sitting-room, so that Julia, coming from the warmth of the hospital, would not feel too much of a chill. Turning on the lights, I found the thermostat, turned it up a few notches, heard the central heating boiler begin to purr, then went to the kitchen and unpacked the basket. I also went quickly round the house, making sure that all was well.

In a way it was fortunate that I did so, for I found that Malcolm's bed had not been made. The Creeds had slept in twin beds, and one of them, which I presumed was his because it had his pyjamas lying on it, was a tumbled mass of sheets and blankets. I imagined that all the time Julia had been in hospital he had not bothered to make the bed for himself, and the sight of it—looking as if he might be just about to climb back into it—would not, I thought, be the best possible thing for Julia. I made it, covering it with the counterpane that had been thrown back at the foot of the bed, and had just started down the stairs when I heard the front doorbell ring.

I went to answer it. I found Sergeant Madden and Jim Baker on the doorstep. A police car was in the road.

"Oh, it's you, Mrs. Freer," the sergeant said. "We had a call at the station that there were lights on in the house. We just came along to make sure there was nothing wrong. It might have got around that the house was empty."

"Would a burglar have turned lights on?" I asked. "Wouldn't he just have prowled around with a torch?"

"You never can tell," he answered. "He might have got it into his head that having the lights blazing would look less suspicious than the odd beam of a torch moving around, if someone was passing and happened to notice it. Not that we really expected trouble, but one has to make sure in a case like this."

They had both stepped into the house and I had closed the door behind them.

"A case like this—don't tell me you think there's something suspicious about Mr. Creed's death," I said. "I mean, is there anything special about it, except for the fact that the driver of the car drove on and got away? You don't think there's any reason why he might have come back to the house?"

"No, none at all," the sergeant said. "It's just as I said, that one has to be sure."

"Do you know who telephoned you?" I asked.

"A Mrs. Greenfield. She said she lives a few doors away and seeing the lights frightened her."

"Yet she's got an army of dogs to protect her," I said.
"Well, I'm sorry you've been troubled."

"You found everything in the house normal, did you?"

"Absolutely."

"Perhaps it would be best if we took a quick look around. We won't be a minute."

Jim looked embarrassed, as if he felt that it looked as if the sergeant was doubting my word, as probably he was. They went quickly over the house, then returned to the hall where I had remained waiting for them.

"I see you've been getting some supplies for Mrs. Creed," the sergeant said as he emerged from the kitchen. "It was you who did it, I take it."

"Yes," I said.

"Very thoughtful of you," he said. "But how did you get in? The place was locked up, I imagine."

"Yes, but I've got a key," I explained. "I've had it for several years. The Creeds always liked me to keep it for them in case they accidentally locked themselves out, and so that I could keep an eye on things for them if they went away. Here it is."

I held it up.

"I see," he said. "A lot of people do that. Good idea really if you've got reliable neighbours. Well, good evening, Mrs. Freer. Lock up carefully when you leave, won't you?"

"Of course."

He and Jim left and I returned to the kitchen, put most of the things that I had bought into the fridge, then returned home.

I found the house empty. Felix was apparently taking his duties as dog-minder seriously, for it was evident that he and Jinks had gone out together for a walk. It was nearly half an hour before they returned. Jinks nosed around my ankles, making sure that I was a person with whom he had some acquaintance. Then he went to the fire in the sitting-room and sat down near it. After a moment he lay down on the hearth-rug and looked as if he had fallen asleep. The poor creature, I thought, was probably very tired. He had suffered an exhausting and probably very bewildering day, apart from having had one ear nearly torn off by a bad-tempered poodle.

"Time for a drink, I think," I said, going to the drinks cupboard. "I don't know about you, but I want whisky this evening."

"You still drink too much," Felix said. "The moment anything out of the ordinary happens to you, you reach for a drink. If you aren't very careful, you'll turn into one of Mrs. Bulpitt's hard cases."

He had always insisted that I drank too much, being himself very temperate, and was as critical of me for this as I was for his smoking.

"You don't want a drink then?" I said as I poured out whisky for myself.

"A rather small sherry," he said. "Virginia . . ." He paused.

"Yes?" I said.

"How would you define blackmail?"

"Oh my God!" I exclaimed. "What have you got on your mind now?"

"Just a passing thought. It's an interesting question really. I happened to start thinking about it as I walked along. How would you define it?"

"Extorting money with menaces, I suppose."

"That's all it is?"

"Isn't that a good deal?"

"Yes, of course. Extorting money with menaces. I see."

I did not. But I did notice that just then Felix would not meet my eyes. He looked very thoughtful and abstracted.

Suddenly I began to wonder why he had taken Jinks for as long a walk as he apparently had. If they had left the house soon after I had gone over to the Creeds', they had been gone a long time. But I did not want to slip into my old habit of worrying about what Felix was up to.

THREE

IT OCCURRED TO ME later that evening that if the girl who was coming to help Julia Creed was to be able to get into the house, I ought to take the key round to Mrs. Bulpitt. But by then I was extremely tired. I was longing for a bath and bed.

My tiredness was not really because I had done such a great deal that day, but more because of the tug on my emotions. The visit to Julia in the morning, all the trouble about poor Jinks in the afternoon, an uncomfortable feeling that Sergeant Madden had not altogether accepted my explanation of what I had been doing in the Creeds' house, even if Jim Baker had, and then the presence of Felix, who seemed to be settling in for a stay of at least some days, left me in a state of nervous tension that made my bones seem to ache and my head feel heavy and confused.

Leaving Felix to look after himself, I went upstairs and had the bath which I so much desired, and for a short time after it, when I had got into my bed, I tried to read a Trollope that I had begun some evenings ago. But even Trollope did not calm me. In the end I took a sleeping-pill, and presently fell into a deep sleep from which I did not waken until eight o'clock next morning.

It was Felix who wakened me, bringing me a cup of tea. Then I got up and went down and made coffee and toast for us both. We had our breakfast as usual in the kitchen, then I told him that I must go round to Mrs. Bulpitt to give her the key to the Creeds' house. He seemed to be in a lugubrious mood.

"I hope it'll work out all right," he muttered, as if he did not think that it would.

"Why shouldn't it?" I said.

"You don't know anything about this girl that woman's got hold of, do you?" he said. "She might be incompetent, she may be crooked, she may be just a bloody bitch."

"Or she may be kind, understanding, and helpful."

"You've more faith in the human species than I have."

"You've got to trust people most of the time, or where would you be?" I asked.

"That's just laziness," he said. "Most of the time we trust people because we can't be bothered not to."

In my time I had trusted Felix himself for a number of other reasons, yet perhaps laziness had had something to do with it. But enchantment had had more. He had been so good-looking, so kind, so entertaining, that it had seemed unnecessary to delve under the surface to find out what might be concealed there. I believe he had a certain contempt for the people who trusted him too readily, even if he felt a more acute dislike for those who did not. He had guessed that Mrs. Bulpitt did not, and he disliked her for it.

"Can we go out to lunch when you've delivered the key?" he asked. "I remember there's that rather good pub in the square—the Rose and Crown, isn't it? Will you come out to lunch with me?"

"I'd like to," I said, "but I've got to go to a party. It's just a drinks party at twelve o'clock and I don't suppose I'll be staying long, but it might make things a bit late for going out to lunch."

He gave a resigned sigh, as if he thought I lived such a hectic social life that he ought to have expected I would refuse to give him a fair share of my time. The party, which had been arranged some days ago, before I had had any reason to expect him to descend on me, was being given by a friend, Janet Gleeson, like me a physio-therapist, who worked at the same clinic as I did. She was married to a doctor and had two children. They lived on the outer edge of the town and I should be going there by car. But first I had to go next door to deliver the Creeds' key to Mrs. Bulpitt.

When about half past nine I rang her doorbell, she came to the door in a grubby quilted dressing-gown and furry, down-at-heel bedroom slippers. Her hair looked as if she had not combed it since getting up.

"The key?" she said when I told her why I had come, but she looked vague, as if she did not understand me. "Oh yes, of course, the key. I'd forgotten all about it. How lucky you thought of it. The Lockett girl said she'd be here about half past ten, which will make me late for church, but of course I shouldn't have been able to let her into the house at all unless I had the key. Come in and have some coffee. I always get up very early and have my breakfast about six o'clock, but I always have some coffee about now. I try to get all my letters written and all my business attended to by then, but today being Sunday of course I've no mail to worry about. But still

I like my coffee. Wasn't it lucky that I was able to get hold of Sue?"

She led me into her sitting-room where there was a tray with coffee on it, just as there had been yesterday when she had been entertaining Felix. She went out to fetch a cup for me.

When she returned, I said, "This girl Sue, you're sure she'll be able to cope?"

"Oh, I should think so," she said. "As I told you, we've had very good reports of her. Not that I really know her myself. I'm not sure I've even met her. But I know we've sent her out on a number of jobs and we've never had any complaints."

Felix had somehow sewn a grain of distrust in my mind.

"Julia will be pretty helpless at first, you know," I said. "I hope the girl's reliable."

"If you're worried about anything, just come and tell me," Mrs. Bulpitt replied, "and I'll see what I can do. It may be easier to find someone after the week-end. But as I said, Sue's done very well—"

She stopped at the sudden sound of something being pushed in at her letter-box.

"Now what can that be?" she said. "Not post on a Sunday. Excuse me a moment."

She got up and went out to the hall. After a moment she returned, holding a package. It was about ten inches by six and done up in brown paper, fastened with Scotch tape.

"Very odd," she remarked, holding it out for me to look at. "It isn't addressed."

"It's nothing you're expecting?" I said.

I had just seen through the window someone walk away up the path to her gate, a tall, slim figure in jeans and a leather jacket, with a helmet on his head. A moment later I heard the roar of a motorcycle as he went away.

"No, perhaps it's a mistake," Mrs. Bulpitt said, "but I think I'll open it. There may be something inside that'll tell me what it is."

She tore at the paper covering the package and ripped it off. Ten-pound notes spilled out of it onto the floor. Lots of them. A whole heap, some of which fell in a lump at her feet, some of which fluttered a little way around her. She gave a gasp and stared at them with a look of incredulous fear. I was sure, just for a moment, that it was fear. Then I began to think that that was absurd and it was simply shock. Then she began to laugh.

The laughter had a shrill note of hysteria in it.

"Money!" she cried. "Lots and lots of lovely money! Shall I keep it? Shall I hide it and not let anyone know I've got it? Oh, my God, if you hadn't been here, that's what I'd do. Lovely, lovely money!"

"You mean it isn't for you?" I said.

"Of course not. How could it be? And here am I, almost desperate for some money, and someone gives me this!"

"Perhaps it is for you," I said. "Who knows you're desperate for money?"

"Oh, everyone! I never make any secret of it. I'm always desperate."

"Then perhaps it's a gift from some wealthy friend who wants to help you out of your difficulties."

"Not likely, the kind of people I know."

"Then perhaps it's a gift for one of your charities."

She gave me a quick, shrewd look. "Perhaps it is, at that. Let's see how much there is."

Her tone had changed. The note of hysteria had gone from

it. She sounded excited but practical. Stooping to gather up
all the notes, she sat down with them in her lap and began to
count them.

After a minute she said, "A thousand. A thousand pounds."

"Is there nothing in the packing that tells you where it
comes from?" I asked.

She picked up the brown paper wrapping she had dropped
on the floor, and carefully took it to pieces.

"Not a thing," she said. "Not a word. And believe me, if
you hadn't been here and seen it happen, I do believe I'd have
quietly hidden it and not tried to find out where it came from
or who it's meant for. Tempting, don't you think? I'm not
above temptation."

"I had a glimpse of the person who delivered it," I said. "I
don't know if it'll mean anything to you."

"Yes?" she said eagerly. "What was he like?"

"I'm afraid I can't tell you much," I said. "A tall, thin
young man in jeans and a leather jacket, wearing one of those
motorcycling helmets. Then I heard the noise of a motorbike
as he rode away."

"Oh," she said. I was not sure if she sounded disappointed
or on the whole satisfied. A curious thought came into my
mind at that moment. Really a preposterous idea. For some
reason that I could not have explained, the memory suddenly
came to me of Felix asking me the evening before how I
would define blackmail, and I actually thought that the
money which had come to Mrs. Bulpitt in such a mysterious
way might be blackmail.

It was only an instant before I dismissed the idea as ridicu-
lous, thinking that the company of Felix had always done
unfortunate things to my powers of judgement. Mrs. Bulpitt's
behaviour had done nothing whatever to support such an

idea. She had evidently been unable to guess where the package had come from. She had not been expecting it. She had opened it in my presence. And although the sight of the money had momentarily excited her, it was obvious that she was very worried by it.

"I'm sure it's an anonymous gift to one of your charities," I said.

"You're probably right," she said soberly. "But why couldn't he say what charity he wanted me to give it to? I'm mixed up in a lot of things."

"I suppose he's leaving that to you."

"Silly fool. Just making things complicated for me."

"I'd treat it as if it had been left entirely to your discretion."

"And you say a young man brought it, a young man in one of those motorcycling helmets?"

"Yes."

"So you didn't see his face. You couldn't describe him."

"No."

"I'm trying to think if I know anyone who rides a motorcycle. One or two, I suppose, but no one with a thousand pounds to throw away. They tend to be the young mostly, don't they, and what menaces they are on the road. Oh . . . !" She put a hand to her mouth as if she were thrusting back some words that had nearly escaped from it.

"I think I know what you were going to say," I said. "Could it be someone who's somehow involved in that accident the other night? But it was a car, you know, that did it. Felix saw most of it, and you and I saw its rear-lights disappearing. There was no motorcycle on the scene."

She nodded thoughtfully. "That's right. There was no motorcycle there. Well, I'd better put this money somewhere safe till I decide what to do with it."

She made it up into a neat bundle and took it out of the room.

I left soon afterwards and went home and tidied myself up for the party to which I was going. I did not feel at all like going to a party. I thought of ringing up to say that I was unavoidably detained at home. But finally I decided that going and not staying long would be the easiest way of coping with the situation. I found Felix stretched out on the sofa in my sitting-room, smoking and reading my Sunday newspaper. Without Sandra to do the job for me I had been too lazy to lay a fire, and Felix had plugged in and switched on the electric radiator. The dog, Jinks, was lying comfortably in front of it, snorting from time to time as if he were having an enjoyable dream.

"What took you so long?" Felix asked, knocking ash from his cigarette on to the hearth. "I thought you were only going to hand her over the key."

"A rather funny thing happened," I said, then wished that I had not as it would only delay my getting changed. "Well, perhaps it was funny, perhaps not. I don't know. Anyway, I'm going out now. I'm not sure when I'll be back. Around half past one, I should think. If you get hungry—"

He interrupted, "What do you mean by funny?"

"Only that while I was there someone pushed a package in at Mrs. Bulpitt's letter-box and when she opened it she found that it contained money. A thousand pounds. And it had no address on it and no indication of who could have sent it, and I'll swear that when she opened it and found what it was she was not only astonished, she was frightened."

"So should I be," Felix said, "if someone suddenly gave me

a thousand pounds without any explanation. It's always frightening, dealing with the insane. We may try to make out we're wise and compassionate, but really we're just scared. Was there really no explanation of where it came from?"

"None at all."

"And she was frightened?"

"I could be wrong about that."

He sat up, tossing the newspaper aside. "All right, let's say you were wrong, but the money came from where?"

"I think someone was giving something anonymously to one of her good causes."

"Without saying which of them it was to go to?"

"So it seems. He just left it to her."

"That's the sort of thing people do when they've a guilty conscience, haven't you noticed? Did you see who brought it?"

"A young man on a motorbike. He had a helmet on, so I can't describe him to you."

"Rum," Felix said. "Very rum. You're sure she was surprised? She wasn't putting on an act?"

"I'm almost certain she was genuinely surprised."

"You see, if really she was expecting it . . ." He paused, frowning thoughtfully at the floor.

"Yes?" I said.

"No, I'm getting sort of mixed up. I'm sure you're right, she wasn't expecting it. For a moment I thought . . . but that's absurd."

"What are you talking about?" I asked.

"Nothing," he said a little too hurriedly. "I did wonder if someone was paying her off for something."

"You mean it was blackmail." Because of the thoughts that I had had in my own mind, I was not entirely surprised.

"No, if it was anything like that she wouldn't have let you see it, would she? I'm sorry, as I said, I'm mixed up. Run along to your party and enjoy yourself."

I did not enjoy myself very much. Usually I liked going to the Gleesons, who gave casual drinks parties fairly often, but I had never before had the thought in my mind of an old friend killed in the street outside my home only two evenings before, of his wife coming home later in the day and most certainly needing a good deal of help, and of Felix waiting for me at home, dropping dark hints about the probity of my neighbour, Mrs. Bulpitt. For even though he had denied it after dropping the hints, I believed he had made up his mind that the package so mysteriously delivered was blackmail connected with the accident in the street.

"Extorting money with menaces . . ."

That had been my own definition of what blackmail was, but why had he wanted me to define it? If the money had come to him it might have been understandable. He might have seen much more of the fatal accident than he had admitted, might have seen the number of the Jaguar and traced its owner, might have threatened to reveal who he was. But with all his peculiarities, I had never known Felix to sink to blackmail. I was fairly certain that he was incapable of it. So what was the explanation?

I knew most of the people who had assembled in the Gleesons' house when I arrived, but there were two strangers there to whom Janet introduced me. They were Dr. and Mrs. Denis Gambrell. I had heard of Dr. Gambrell from people in the clinic where I worked. He had come to Allingford about two years ago and was a gynaecologist, a consultant in St. Mary's Hospital, but I had never met him before. He was about fifty, a man of medium height, square-shouldered, heavily built, going a little bald but with a smooth, pink, unwrinkled face and slightly bulging, very shrewd grey eyes. His wife, Harriet, looked a little younger than he did, was tall, very slender, auburn-haired, and dressed in close-fitting emerald green which looked elegant and expensive.

It was Dr. Gambrell who started talking to me about the accident in Ellsworthy Street. Apparently he and his wife had read of it in a local paper.

"He was done for immediately, it said," he observed. "He hadn't a hope."

"No," I said.

"It was someone you knew?"

"Yes, a neighbour of mine who lived across the street. A Mr. Creed. It happened almost in front of my house."

"What was he?"

"He was retired," I said. "I believe he'd been in the RAF and then tried farming in Kenya, but gave it up and settled here. He was about eighty, I think, and so is his wife, who's been in St. Mary's for the last week or two and is coming home today."

"Oh, the poor woman!" Mrs. Gambrell said. "But she knows . . . I mean, she has been told her husband's been killed?"

"Oh yes," I said.

"Doesn't a Mrs. Bulpitt live in Ellsworthy Street?" the doctor asked.

"Yes, she's my next-door neighbour," I said. "Do you know her?"

"We've met," he said. "She's on one of the committees I have to belong to. She's a very worthy woman."

"Very," I agreed.

"Personally, I can't bear her," Mrs. Gambrell said and gave

a little titter, though also giving me a sharp glance to see how I would take this. "I remember the first time I met her I thought no, we aren't going to be friends. One of these chemical things. We're both on the committee of a group called Help in Need. I don't mean I've anything against her. She's a friend of yours, is she?"

I did not mean to hesitate in replying, but then I said, "Yes, we get on very well."

"Do they know who was driving the car that killed Creed?" Dr. Gambrell asked.

"I don't believe so," I said.

"It didn't stop, then?"

"No."

"Bad business. Shocking."

At that point Janet Gleeson came up to refill our glasses, the Gambrells moved away, and I started talking to an old friend about some amateur theatricals in which she was involved. Soon afterwards I said good-bye to Janet and her husband and made for home.

As I drove, I think I was thinking more about the dress that Mrs. Gambrell had been wearing than I was about the death of Malcolm Creed. For the first time since his death, something else had jostled it out of my mind. She was the kind of smart woman who always intimidates me far more than someone whom I would have called beautiful. Actually I use the word beautiful very sparingly. Good-looking, charming, attractive, fascinating, all are words that I apply to a good many people, as often to men as to women, but the number of people whom I have known and have called beautiful is remarkably small.

But if it was possible to buy in Allingford the kind of dress that Mrs. Gambrell had been wearing, I should have liked to know where. However, she struck me as the kind of woman who would make a secret of a thing like that, just as she would probably be ungenerous about sharing her more successful recipes even with her best friends. And anyway the dress had probably come from London. I was still thinking about this when I drove past Mrs. Bulpitt's house and saw a man coming out of it.

There was nothing remarkable about this except that I had a feeling I had seen him before, yet I could not remember where or when, and this worried me. He was a very thin man, about six feet tall, wearing a loose raincoat. I thought that he was about thirty-five or forty. Possibly, I thought, he was one of the policemen who had been in the street after the accident and it was because I had caught sight of him then that he seemed familiar now. But they had all been uniformed men. Could this man be a detective, and if so, what was there about the death of Malcolm Creed that would bring a plain-clothes officer to the scene of it? But very likely I was wrong and he had nothing to do with the police. I did not pause to get a good look at him, but drove on past the house and turned in at my garage.

As I went into the house I smelled cigarette smoke, which meant that Felix was still there, as well as a very pleasant aroma of something cooking. It was curry, I thought. Felix had always been an adept at curries. He must have taken some chicken out of my freezer and got to work cooking to fill in the time while I was gone. He was in the kitchen with Jinks. The dog came waddling out as I opened the front door and gave a half-hearted bark at me, as if I were an intruder, then went into the sitting-room and settled himself down again in front of the electric fire.

"Had a good time?" Felix asked me as I went into the kitchen.

"Not particularly," I said.

"What was wrong?"

"Nothing specially."

He glanced at me as he stood at the stove.

"You aren't wearing your ear-rings," he said.

"No."

"Don't you like them?"

"I do, very much."

"Then why didn't you put them on?"

"I don't know." In fact, I had not thought of them. I suppose I must have been a little afraid to appear in them in public in case someone who saw them might be able to make a guess at where they had come from, and so I had conveniently forgotten them. "Felix, before I went out we were talking about blackmail."

"So we were." He was beginning to spoon rice and curry on to two plates.

"And yesterday evening you asked me to define blackmail."

"Did I? Yes, I believe I did."

"You know you did."

"And you said it was extorting money with menaces. So if there weren't any menaces involved, it couldn't be blackmail, could it?"

"Of course not. But I don't really know what you're talking about."

"And if there was no money involved, it couldn't be blackmail either?"

"In fact, if nothing at all happened, it couldn't be blackmail; I think we might accept that as certain."

"But of course there's that mysterious thing people call emotional blackmail, isn't there?" he said. "No one actually threatens anything, no money changes hands, but one calls it blackmail."

"But it was my telling you about Mrs. Bulpitt getting that strange thousand pounds that started you talking about blackmail this morning," I said. "You said someone could be paying her off. You think she knows something about that acci- dent on Friday."

"I shouldn't be surprised if she does, but her getting that money may have nothing to do with it."

"You haven't been trying a little blackmail yourself, Felix, have you? Suppose the money had simply been delivered to the wrong door and ought to have been delivered here. The young man on the motorbike might simply have been an errand boy and got the wrong address." I had thought of this possibility on my drive home from the Gleesons' party. "Is that it? Did you really see the number of the car and have you been putting pressure on someone? You could have done some telephoning while I was out at the hospital yesterday."

He slammed the two plates of curry and rice down on the kitchen table. There was a very bitter look on his face.

"What do you take me for?" he demanded. "If I really knew who killed that poor devil in the street and drove off, do you think I'd let him get away with paying me a mere thousand pounds?"

"I'm sorry," I said. "I don't really believe you've ever blackmailed anybody, but you must admit it's a pretty theory."

"All the same," he said as we sat down at the table, "it happens that I do know who the driver of the car was."

"Felix!" I stared at him helplessly. "You don't mean that."

"As a matter of fact, I do."

"Then why haven't you told the police?"

"Because I haven't any evidence that's absolutely positive. I've felt nearly a hundred percent certain since you told me about that money being delivered to Mrs. Bulpitt, but it's nothing that would stand up in a court of law."

"You haven't got to stand up in a court of law. You wouldn't be under oath. You'd merely be telling the police something that they might find helpful."

"Well, I'll think about it."

An expression appeared on his face which meant, I knew, that he was prepared to ignore my existence and intended to devote himself solely to his curry. It seemed best to me that I should do this too.

Later in the afternoon I went over to the Creeds' house. I did not go immediately after lunch because it seemed to me probable that when Julia arrived from the hospital she would want a rest, but I wanted to see what sort of a girl Sue Lockett was and whether Julia would be safe in her hands. It was about four o'clock when I rang the bell and the door was opened to me.

It was not a girl but a young man who opened it. He was tall, wide-shouldered, narrow-hipped, and had a lounging kind of grace. He had fair hair standing up in a tuft above his forehead, a pale, pointed face with high cheekbones, and eyes of a remarkable blue. But one of these eyes, it was interesting to note, had been well blackened. He had recently collided with something, whether it was merely a lamp-post or, more probably, a well-aimed fist. He was in the universal uniform of the young, jeans and a T-shirt. I thought that he was in his early twenties.

"Hallo," he said, "you want Sue?"

"Please," I said.

"You're who?" he asked.

"My name's Freer," I said. "I live across the road."

"I'm Simon Prescott," he said. "Friend of Sue's. I brought her. Must be going soon, just wanted to see her settled in. Looks as if it'll be okay. The old lady's very nice."

He had not yet invited me into the house. Turning in the doorway, he shouted over his shoulder. "Sue!"

A girl came hurrying down the stairs. Like the boy, she was wearing jeans and a T-shirt. She had a long, narrow face with strong, somewhat heavy features, big dark eyes and a square, determined chin. Her hair was dark brown, tied back in a pony-tail with what looked like a shoe-lace.

"Ssh!" she said fiercely. "There's no need to make such a row. She's just settling down nicely with a book." She turned to me. "Yes?" Like him, she did not seem to expect me to come in.

"I'm Mrs. Freer from across the road," I said. "I'm a friend of Mrs. Creed. I called in to see if she's all right and to ask if there's anything I can do."

She hesitated, then pushed the boy to one side and gestured to me to enter.

"Thanks," she said, "but I can manage. But if you'd like to see her—that is, if she'd like to see you—she's lying down upstairs. Simon, you can go. You can give me a ring later, if you like."

"Okay." He kissed her on the cheek, then picked up a leather jacket from a chair in the hall and shrugged it on.

As he went out I suddenly thought that, except for the absence of a helmet, he might have been the young man who had pushed the package containing a thousand pounds in at Mrs. Bulpitt's door in the morning. But the young all look so alike nowadays that there was no real reason to assume that that was who he was, and it was not on a motorcycle that he left, but in an ancient and battered Vauxhall which had been standing at the gate.

"If you'll wait a minute I'll go up and tell her you're here," the girl said. "I can't say for sure if she'll want to see anyone. She's all right one minute, then crying her eyes out the next. Can you wonder? But it was all over in a moment, I believe, so he didn't suffer. I don't suppose he knew what hit him."

I remembered the hoarse scream that I had heard as I went to answer my telephone, and thought that Malcolm Creed must have had at least one moment of terror and perhaps of agony, but it was true that it must have been over quickly. The girl did not sound particularly concerned, but going from one home where there was trouble to the next, as she must do in her work, she had no doubt become somewhat hardened. And that might, for all I knew, be best for her various employers. Remaining relatively uninvolved and impersonal might make her most useful.

She turned towards the stairs, but paused before going up.

"Did you see the accident?" she asked.

"No," I said.

"Funny thing, I've never seen an accident, not once," she said. "Yet they're happening all the time. I tell Simon, the way he drives, he's bound to be in one sooner or later, but you can't talk sense into his head. He's always getting into trouble. You notice his black eye?"

"I did, as a matter of fact," I said.

"Got it in a brawl in a pub last night," she said. "Bloody fool. I'll pop up and see if Mrs. Creed feels like a visitor. Shan't be a minute."

She shot off up the stairs.

She was back again almost at once and told me that Mrs. Creed would be glad to see me. I went upstairs, found the door to Julia's bedroom standing open, and went in. She was lying on her bed, not actually in it, and was wearing the pale blue dressing-gown in which I had seen her in the hospital. A book was lying flat on her stomach. If she had tried to read, she had not gone on for long. Her eyes were red and there were the streaks of tears on her hollow cheeks. She had a handkerchief clutched in one hand. It looked a very big hand-kerchief. One of Malcolm's, I thought.

I sat down on the edge of the other bed in the room.

"How are you?" I asked.

"Fine," she answered as automatically as if I had dropped a coin into her somewhere and the response had come out. "Fine."

"You're feeling quite well?"

"Oh yes, quite well."

"Julia, can I help in any way?"

She gave a deep sigh. "It's nice of you to ask, dear, but really there's nothing anyone can do, is there? I've just got to get used to things. I suppose one does get used to things in the end. Other people have to. Only it makes me feel I wish I hadn't come through that operation. That would have made everything simpler. Fifty-seven years we were married, you know."

I thought of all sorts of trite things to say in answer, but in the end was silent.

After a moment she picked up the book that was lying on her stomach, closed it, and put it down on the bedside table.

"It's no use, I can't read," she said. "That girl tried to make me. She said it would do me good. But when I've read about a line my mind begins to wander. I don't want television either."

"How do you like her?" I asked.

"The girl? I suppose she's all right."

There was something grudging in her tone which made me say, "What's the trouble?"

"Oh, no trouble really," she said. "I'm sure she's doing her best. After all, she hasn't found her way about yet. She brought me a huge plate of food for lunch and I could hardly touch it. And when she saw I hadn't she got—well, I won't say rude, but quite offended, or upset, or something. I said I was very sorry when she'd gone to all the trouble of getting it, and she said there was no pleasing some people and I needn't worry, she wouldn't do it again."

"So she's a bit of a bully, is she?"

"I think so. Used to having her own way at least. But honestly, I couldn't have eaten a quarter of what she'd brought. I didn't meant to be unappreciative."

"I shouldn't worry about it," I said. "She'll find out where she is in a little while."

"I only wish I was strong enough to look after myself. I'd like best to be alone. Actually I believe I could manage all right if I had to. I don't mean I don't want to see you, dear, it's sweet of you to come, but I don't like being pushed around. Only I don't feel up to arguing with her."

"I'll have a word with her, if you like," I said. "I'll just tell her to let you take things slowly."

"Oh no, don't do that. She might think I'd been criticizing her. But I'll tell you another thing about her. I do wish she wouldn't wear those awful jeans and that sloppy jumper. But please don't say anything about that either. I know it's what they all do nowadays. But she'd look so much nicer in a pretty little dress, wouldn't she? Not that she's exactly pretty herself. That thick nose and the little mouth with the big teeth— Still, I can't help feeling there's something almost ill-mannered in coming to a stranger's house in something so informal. It wouldn't be so bad if the trousers only fitted."

It was plain that, for whatever reason, Sue Lockett did not suit Julia Creed. I wondered if there was anything that I could do about it.

"I'm sorry you don't like her," I said. "Mrs. Bulpitt got hold of her for us at very short notice, and said they'd had very good reports of her."

"Oh, I don't want you to think I don't like her," she said. "I'm sure I'm just being difficult and it's my fault. Have you met that young man of hers?"

"Just for a moment."

"He's got a black eye, hasn't he?"

"That's how it looks. Sue said he'd been in a brawl in a pub."

"Imagine! Do you think . . . ?" She paused.

"Yes?" I said.

"Well, you know what the young are like these days. Do you think that they're—oh, I don't know quite how to put it, but do you think they're 'living together'?" Her voice dropped into a whisper at the end of the sentence.

"Not improbably," I said.

"But do you think—I know one isn't supposed to worry about these things anymore—but do you think he'll be coming here to spend the night? Because I shouldn't like that, Virginia. I mean, the sort of young man who gets into brawls in pubs, I really wouldn't like to think he was roaming about the house."

I saw her point and began to think that I might call in on

Mrs. Bulpitt to ask her if in any reports that she had had of Sue Lockett there had ever been any mention of an attendant boy-friend.

However, I said, "I shouldn't worry about that. Even if he comes, which I don't really think is likely, I think she'll be able to keep him in order. From the way she spoke of it to me, I don't think she approves of his brawling."

Julia nodded her head. "And of course she's very strong-minded. I'm sure I've nothing to worry about."

I got up to leave.

"If anything happens that worries you," I said, "you've only got to telephone us."

"Us?" she said, puzzled. "Have you someone staying with you?"

"Oh, I didn't tell you, did I?" I said. "My husband's come home for the moment."

She managed a smile of sorts, though it was not much more than a strange-looking grimace on her stricken face.

"Isn't that nice!" she said. "Are you thinking of making things up? That would be so nice."

"I'm not sure that it would be unless he'd change some of his ways, but it's quite pleasant to have him here once in a while."

"Malcolm and I were married for fifty-seven years—oh, I told you that, didn't I—and I don't think we ever had a serious quarrel. Just a little bickering now and then about things that didn't matter in the least. Well, it was very nice of you to come, dear. Thank you for it."

"Shall I look in tomorrow, or would that be a nuisance?"

"Oh no, do look in. I'll look forward to it."

I gave her a kiss and then left her.

I did not see Sue Lockett again on my way out, though I

heard her at work of some sort in the kitchen. I called out good-bye, to which she did not reply, then I went home, turning over in my mind what I ought to do. Felix was lying on the sofa once more when I got in. He looked asleep, but as I closed the door of the sitting-room behind me and crossed the room towards the fireplace, he opened his eyes and watched me without moving anything but his eyelids. Then he roused himself sufficiently to reach for a cigarette.

"All well?" he asked.

"I'm not sure," I answered. "Julia's taken a dislike to the girl, but I'm not sure if that's just an inevitable sort of irritability which she'd feel towards anyone at the moment, however angelic they were, or if there's really something wrong. I think I'm going next door to ask Mrs. Bulpitt how much she really knows about the girl."

"Didn't you see her yourself?"

"Just briefly."

"And what did you feel?"

"I wasn't drawn to her. But Julia's got to have help of some sort. She's still very weak, and this arrangement may work once she and Sue have got used to one another. I'll go round to Mrs. Bulpitt now. I don't expect I'll be long."

He swung his legs down to the floor. "I'll be getting some tea."

I left him to do it and went next door.

There was no answer when I rang Mrs. Bulpitt's bell, though I could hear it ringing inside the house. She might be having an afternoon nap, I thought, or unluckily be out. I rang the bell again and there was still no answer. So I was turning away, thinking that I would have to try again sometime in the evening, when I noticed that the front door was not completely closed. I put a hand on it and it swung open.

I hesitated, then put my head inside and called out, "Mrs. Bulpitt!"

There was no answer. I called again, then took a step into the house and stood there, uncertain what to do. If she had left the door ajar intentionally, it might mean that she had gone out without a key and if I closed it she would find herself locked out. But if it was accidental and she was in fact lying down upstairs, or perhaps had gone out for some time, it might be best to close the door. I took a step forward.

It was at that moment, through the open door of the kitchen, that I saw a foot in a down-at-heel brown shoe and part of a leg lying on the floor.

I ran forward. I am not sure what I expected to find. That she had had a stroke, or had fallen and knocked herself unconscious, or even that she might be dead drunk and had passed out, though I had never had any evidence that she was a secret drinker.

She was certainly dead, but drink had had nothing to do with it. She was lying collapsed on the greasy-looking linoleum with her eyes glaring fiercely at the ceiling and her head in a pool of blood.

FOUR

MY FIRST IMPULSE was to run from the house, probably screaming, to get hold of Felix, who practically never lost his head in any crisis. But before I had actually done this I realised that the first thing I ought to do was call the police. There was a telephone in the sitting-room and I went to it and dialled 999. When I found myself talking to someone who said he was a sergeant, it might even have been Sergeant Madden, I told him who I was, where I was, and that I had discovered a murder.

He told me that the police would be round in a few minutes. That meant, I realised as I put the telephone down, that I would have to remain where I was until the police arrived. I could not go home. But there was nothing to stop me telephoning Felix.

When he answered, I told him what had happened and he said that he would be round immediately.

"But don't touch anything," he said. "Be very careful not to touch anything."

As I put the telephone down I began to consider what I had touched. The telephone, of course. And the front door as I had pushed it open. But nothing else that I could remember.

I was not sure why it was so important that I should touch nothing, except that a point is always made of this in detective stories and Felix read a great many of them. But I supposed it made sense that if someone else who had been in the house and probably killed Mrs. Bulpitt by smashing her skull, had left his fingerprints anywhere, I should be careful not to superimpose mine on his, disguising them.

Standing by the telephone, I felt unable to move away from it, as if it were my link with the normal world. But then I began to look around me and the first thing that caught my eye was a photograph. I believe that unconsciously I had been looking for it, because it was somewhere lodged in my memory. I had seen it often. It was in a narrow black frame standing on the mantelpiece, and was of a young man, probably in his mid-twenties, with a fairly handsome but commonplace face, not arresting in any way. Yet it arrested me. It was the face of the man whom I had seen coming out of Mrs. Bulpitt's house when I was returning from the Gleesons' party.

That explained why that man's face had seemed familiar. It was simply because I knew the picture so well. I had never asked Mrs. Bulpitt who he was, and as she had a number of photographs, mostly of young women, scattered about the room, I had always assumed that they must be children or grandchildren. Perhaps he was even a son. Yet she had never mentioned having a son. She had never mentioned anything to speak of about her family.

It is extraordinary how difficult it is not to touch anything when you have been told that you must not. If I had not been told this, I believe that I should have thrust my hands into the pockets of my overcoat and stayed almost still. But as it was, I had the greatest difficulty in restraining myself from grasping the back of a chair near the telephone and slightly altering its position, and in not picking up a newspaper that lay on the floor and putting it neatly on a table, and in not going to the photograph of the young man on the mantelpiece and picking it up and looking at it more closely than I ever had before.

I managed to control myself, but it was a strain, and I did go to the fireplace and study the photograph from only a foot or so away, asking myself if I really was quite sure that it was the man whom I had seen come out of the house. The more carefully I studied the photograph the less sure I was, but that of course could be a simple case of first impressions being the most reliable. I was just turning away, unconvinced, when I heard Felix come in at the front door, which I had left open behind me.

He called out, "Virginia!"

I went out into the hall to meet him.

He took me in his arms, which was unusual, and said, "Are you all right?"

Until that moment this was a matter that I had not thought about, but as soon as he asked the question I came to the conclusion that I was not all right at all, and that I was in a state of acute shock.

"In there," I said and pointed at the kitchen doorway.

He went to it and stood there, looking in. I heard him draw two or three deep breaths.

"This is a hell of a thing," he said. "I was thinking of going home tomorrow."

"You can still go," I said.

"The police may say they'd sooner I didn't. And by tomorrow you may be feeling too you'd sooner I didn't."

"You can't do anything by staying here."

"You can't be sure."

"You didn't see anything suspicious while I was out, did you?"

"Not a thing."

"Then why should you stay?" It was absurd, but I was arguing against myself. I wanted him very badly to stay, but the more I wanted it the more I felt impelled to persuade him to leave. Of course I knew that he would not.

"I expect they'll send us home when they get here," he said. "We're as accessible as if we stay here and we shan't be under their feet. And you look as if some whisky wouldn't come amiss."

That, in fact, was how things happened when the first instalment of the police arrived a few minutes later. As before, it was Sergeant Madden and Jim Baker, but we understood that there were far bigger guns to come. Sergeant Madden took a very brief statement from me of how I happened to have discovered the murder, then himself suggested that Felix and I should return next door, but keep ourselves available for when the superintendent arrived.

Thankfully, we left. Jinks was in the hall and put up a show of barking at us when we let ourselves into the house, then, as I collapsed in a chair in the sitting-room and said to Felix, "That whisky, please!" the old dog tottered up to me and laid his head on my knee. He looked bewildered and sad, but ready on the whole to accept us as friends.

Felix mixed a very strong whisky for me, but himself stuck to sherry.

It was nearly an hour before Detective Superintendent Dawnay arrived at my door. It was dark by then and Felix had drawn the sitting-room curtains, shutting out our sight of all the police cars that had arrived in the street and all the coming and going of men, mostly in plain clothes. But we could hear through the not-very-thick wall that divided Mrs. Bulpitt's house from mine, heavy footsteps on the staircase, occasional loud voices, and the sound of continuing activity.

Listening to it and sipping my whisky, I asked Felix, "How long do you think she'd been dead?"

"I haven't the slightest idea," he answered.

"No, of course not," I said. "It was a silly question."

"The last you saw of her was in the morning, wasn't it, when you took round the key?" he said.

"Yes, but I suppose the girl, Sue Lockett, across the road, saw her after that, as she must have collected the key. And Mrs. Bulpitt spoke as if she was going out to church, so she may have been seen there."

"All the same it looks as if she may have been killed sometime in the morning."

I thought again of the man in the raincoat whom I had seen come out of Mrs. Bulpitt's house as I returned from the Gleesons. That must have been about half past one. But I said, "That may not mean anything."

It was then that my doorbell rang and Felix went to answer it, returning with Detective Superintendent Dawnay and a Sergeant Wells, who introduced themselves and accepted chairs. Then the superintendent began to question me.

He was about forty-five, I thought, not as tall as one usually expects policemen to be, and so slenderly built that I could not believe he could be very useful in a punch-up. Yet there was an alertness about him, a natural lightness of movement that implied very well-coordinated muscles. He had thick, dark brown hair, and skin dark enough to make his singularly pale grey eyes look almost colourless.

The sergeant was a big, burly man with rough fair hair, a

reddish face, and blunt features which looked as if a punch-up was just what they were made for. He had a notebook, and as the superintendent began to talk to me, he started rapidly making notes in shorthand.

"I've talked to Sergeant Madden," Superintendent Dawnay said, "and he's told me it was you who found the body and phoned the police. Can you tell me how that happened?"

"I went to see Mrs. Bulpitt to consult her about something," I said. "I went round and got no answer when I rang, but I noticed the door wasn't quite closed and I went in and called out to her and then—then I saw her. The kitchen door was open."

"You knew her well, then?" he asked.

"Fairly well. We've been neighbours for a couple of years."

"This thing you wanted to consult her about, can you explain that?"

"It's a bit complicated," I said, "but it was about a girl—a girl called Sue Lockett—who Mrs. Bulpitt had got hold of to help a friend of ours across the road, a Mrs. Creed, who was expected home from hospital today, and who really isn't fit to look after herself. Mrs. Bulpitt managed to get hold of the girl because she works in an organization called Help in Need, who supply people to do just that kind of thing. And I'd been over to see Mrs. Creed to make sure that things were working out all right, and I found . . ."

"Yes, you found?" he said as I stopped. His colourless eyes were intently fixed on my face.

"Only that things didn't seem too satisfactory," I said. "Mrs. Creed seemed to have taken a dislike to the girl. Probably quite unreasonably. She's been fairly seriously ill and then had the awful shock of her husband's death—you know about that, I suppose."

"Yes." That seemed to be all that he intended to say about it.

"Well, as I was going to say," I went on, "her dislike could have been just an invalid's irritability, but I thought I'd look in on Mrs. Bulpitt and ask her how much she really knew about the girl. That was all."

"And this happened about when?"

I seemed to have lost count of time for the last hour or two, but peering apparently thoughtfully, though really sightlessly, at my watch, I said, "Sometime between half past four and five, I should think."

Felix said, "Do you know yet when the murder happened, Superintendent?"

"Not really," Dawnay answered. "The forensic people have made a rough guess that it may have been sometime between twelve and two o'clock. They may be able to tell us more when they've got around to the post-mortem."

"Oh, in that case . . . !" I exclaimed, then stopped again.

He again said, "Yes?"

"It's only that at about half past one I drove past Mrs. Bulpitt's house," I said. "I was on my way home from having drinks with friends and as I was passing her house I saw a man come out. I had a funny feeling at the time that I'd seen him before, but I didn't get a good look at him. There was no reason at the time why I should pay any special attention to him. But later . . ." Thinking of what had happened later made me pause uneasily. "I could be quite wrong, you see," I went on, "but later, in her sitting-room, I looked at the photograph of a young man that she's got on her mantelpiece and I thought that that was who the man had been whom I'd seen come out. He looked a good bit older than he does in the photograph, but I think it was the same man."

"And who was he?" Dawnay asked.

"I don't know," I said.

"Did she never say who the photograph was of?"

I shook my head.

"Never mentioned a son, or a brother, or a husband, or anyone?"

"I can't remember that she did."

"The room's full of photographs," he said.

"Yes."

"But you never asked who any of the people were?"

"No, they didn't mean anything to me. Some people hoard photographs of almost everyone they've ever met. They aren't interesting to anyone else."

"I think we know who some of the people are," he said with a disconcerting little smile, as if there were something comic about my knowing nothing about them. "This party you went to, Mrs. Freer, where was that?"

It was only after I had answered that it had been at Dr. Gleeson's that it occurred to me that he was asking me for an alibi. But of course I had no alibi. If Mrs. Bulpitt could have been murdered as late as two o'clock, I had returned home, according to my own admission, before that. And so far as I knew, Felix had been at home all the morning, though there might be no one who could corroborate that.

He had not sat down when the others had, but was standing near the window with his hands clasped behind him.

"Virginia, don't you think you should tell Mr. Dawnay about the thousand pounds?" he said.

It startled me to realize that I had virtually forgotten about the mysteriously delivered thousand pounds.

"A thousand pounds?" the superintendent said.

"Yes, it was a rather strange thing that happened this morning," I said. "I'd gone over to see Mrs. Bulpitt to give her the key of Mrs. Creed's house, because the girl she'd got hold of would have gone to her for it. And we had coffee together and while we were having it we heard something pushed in at her letter-box. And it was a package done up in brown paper without any address on it, and when she opened it she found it contained a thousand pounds in ten-pound notes. And there was nothing inside to show who it had come from and she seemed completely astonished. I believe she really was astonished. I'm sure her surprise was genuine. And we talked about it and rather came to the conclusion, though I think it may have been my idea rather than hers, that it was an anonymous donation to one of the charities she's mixed up with. I'm not sure if she really believed that, but she hadn't any other suggestion. I had a glimpse through the window of the man who'd delivered the package. He was tall and thin and was dressed in jeans and a leather jacket and had a motorcycling helmet on, and he went away on a motorbike."

At first Dawnay said nothing. He looked at me attentively, as if he were waiting to see if any more was coming, while the sergeant scribbled frantically in his notebook.

Dawnay said, "A thousand pounds. What did she do with it? Just left it lying somewhere there?"

"No, she said she was going to put it somewhere safe," I said, "and she took it out of the room. I don't know where she put it."

"You're sure of that? She didn't leave it in the sitting-room?"

"I'm quite sure," I said.

"A pity," he said. "We haven't really searched the house

yet and so far we haven't found any bundle of ten-pound notes, but if only it had been in some obvious place and now gone missing it would have supplied us with such a simple motive for her murder. Murders are often committed for much less than a thousand pounds."

"Have you any idea yet about the motive?" Felix asked.

"Nothing substantial," Dawnay answered. "We've hardly begun on the case and aren't jumping to conclusions. But what your wife has just told me may be very important."

It always gives me a strange feeling to hear myself described as Felix's wife, though of course this is strictly accurate.

"I don't know what she'd have done with the money in the end," I said. "She made a bit of a joke of the idea that she'd have kept it for herself if I hadn't been there to see her get it. She talked of being desperate for money and I asked her who knew this, because I wondered if it was possible that one of the fairly wealthy people who work on the same good causes as she did might be trying to help her out. But she didn't seem to think much of my idea."

"The interesting thing is that she wasn't desperate for money," Dawnay said. "She was a moderately rich woman."

I stared at him in surprise, and he stared steadily back with those pale eyes that seemed to have no expression in them.

"Oh yes," he said. "We haven't had time to do a thorough search of the house, though we'll certainly get on with it now that we know about that thousand pounds, but we came on her last month's bank statement in the drawer of a bureau in her sitting-room, and she's got a little over two thousand in her current account. And in a special reserve account she's got ninety-seven thousand pounds."

"Ninety-seven *thousand?*" I exclaimed, thinking that he

must have got confused and said thousands when he meant hundreds.

"Oh yes," he said, "and she's got share certificates in another drawer of the bureau which I've only glanced at so far, but I should think she'd got something approaching half a million altogether."

"That can't be right," I said. "I *know* she was very hard up. Look at her house. She always said she couldn't afford to have anyone in to clean it and that she was too old to cope with it herself, and so it got in the state it did. And I don't know if you looked at her clothes yet, but everything she had was ancient and probably very cheap in the first place."

"Actually she had some rather remarkable clothes," he said. "Among other things, she'd several lavish evening dresses. A bit dated, I've been told by one of our constables who knows more about such things than I do, but certainly costly. And she'd a lot of high-heeled, obviously very expensive shoes, mostly Italian. They were hardly worn. It looks as if for some reason, not so very long ago, she completely changed her lifestyle."

"Were there any cosmetics in her room?" Felix asked.

"Yes, a fair amount, all the most expensive brands," Dawnay answered.

"But she never wore make-up at all!" I protested.

He gave a little shrug of his shoulders.

"And she's got half a million?" I said.

"Just about."

"Then I suppose she was a miser, wasn't she?"

"That's how it looks."

"And someone may have known this. Someone may have known how to get money out of her."

"It's one of the possibilities we've got to bear in mind."

"Do you know where her money came from?"

Just for a moment he lowered his eyes, and with the experience behind me of all the years of knowing Felix, I felt a second's absolute certainty that I was about to be told a lie. But in the end, as he looked back at me, it was only an evasion.

"Mrs. Freer, we've hardly begun on this case. What you've told us has been very useful, but we're still almost completely in the dark."

So he did know where the money came from, I thought, but he was letting me know that I need not expect him to tell me anything about it. He and the sergeant left after that and I immediately helped myself to more whisky. Felix muttered that I was half-way to becoming an alcoholic, then asked what we were going to eat that evening.

I had not given the matter a thought and I did not feel like doing so now. I felt as if it would probably be hours before I began to feel like thinking about food. But Felix likes regular meals, even when he has to prepare them himself, and fortunately is an excellent cook. He decided that he would make us omelettes that evening and wanted to know if I had any mushrooms in the house. As it happened I had, so he left me to myself while he went out to the kitchen to cook them. I sat there, sipping my whisky and brooding on the astonishing fact that my neighbour, Mrs. Bulpitt, who had seemed to me the most honest of women, the most concerned with the troubles of others, the most entirely free from vices, had in fact suffered from that most unattractive of them: she had been a miser.

Yet this could not always have been so, if it was true about the evening dresses and the shoes and the cosmetics. Something must have happened to her to make her change her way

of life so completely. Could she have had a mental breakdown, I wondered? Could she perhaps have suffered some
great loss which had entirely changed her view of how life
should be lived? I had never thought much about Mr.
Bulpitt. He had always seemed to belong entirely to a not-
very-important past. But could I have been quite wrong
about this, and could his death have dealt her a blow from
which she had never wholly recovered, and left her a miser,
living in secret a fantasy life of glamour?

I was pondering this when the front doorbell rang.

I took for granted it was the police again, wanting to tell
me or to ask me something more about that thousand pounds.
But I was wrong. It was Julia Creed. She was in an overcoat
which she kept clasped about her so closely that I thought it
was possible that under it she was not fully dressed. She was
wearing red velvet bedroom slippers, not shoes, and was
clutching a walking-stick.

"Thank goodness you're at home," she said. "I'm so worried. I don't know what to do."

I drew her quickly into the house and took her to a chair
beside the electric fire in the sitting-room. She still held her
coat closely about her.

"What's happened?" I asked.

"I only wish I knew," she answered. "It's so upsetting. But
tell me, all those police in the street and the cars and the
ambulance, that can't have anything to do with Malcolm, can
it? I mean, why should they want an ambulance now?"

She was interrupted by Jinks, who leapt up to her with the
joy of recognition, licking her face, then doing his best to
settle on her lap. She stroked him in an absent-minded way,
looking at me with wide, bewildered eyes.

"No, it's nothing to do with Malcolm," I said. "Something

has happened . . . But why did you come over, Julia? You aren't fit to be out. If you'd telephoned I could have come over to you."

"Yes, I suppose you could. I didn't think of it." She pushed the dog off her lap, but he stayed close to her, rubbing himself against her legs. "Poor old Jinks," she said. "You don't mind looking after him for me for the moment, do you, Virginia?"

"Not in the least," I said. "He's no trouble."

"I suppose he'll have to be put down. I can't see myself being able to take care of him, taking him for his little walks and all. But it's very sad. Malcolm was very fond of him."

I wished that she had said simply that the dog would have to be killed, rather than "put down," which is a meaningless phrase. I always recoil from expressions of that sort, such as the statement that someone has passed on, or passed over. There is dignity in the word "death," which should not be disguised by euphemisms.

"Would you like a drink?" I asked. "Or some tea?"

"No, thank you, nothing," she said. "I've had some tea. And that's how it happened. It's really so strange. Oh . . . !" This exclamation was because Felix had just appeared at the door of the sitting-room. Evidently he had heard our voices and had abandoned his mushroom omelettes for the present. Julia wrapped her overcoat even more closely about her, as if she were afraid that she might be caught out in immodesty. "I didn't know you had a visitor," she said.

"It's only Felix," I said. "As I told you, he drops in sometimes. Felix, this is Mrs. Creed."

He advanced into the room and shook hands with her. She gave him a bemused stare, then looked down at Jinks and

began to stroke his head, as if the mere fact that he and she
were long acquainted gave her some feeling of security.

"Of course, I ought to have telephoned," she said, "but
with all those police out there and not knowing what was
going on, I got frightened of being alone and thought I'd
rush over. Perhaps it was silly. Perhaps I'm not really up to it
yet. It's made me feel sort of shaky. But that house feels so
big and empty."

"Alone?" I said. "But haven't you got Sue Lockett there?"

"No, she's gone." She was still looking down at Jinks and
stroking him, but she gave a sharp little shiver as she said it.

"Gone altogether, do you mean?" I asked. "Or just gone
out to see someone or something?"

"Oh no, gone away altogether," she said. "She got me my
tea downstairs, then told me she thought I should go up to
bed when I'd had it as I'd done enough for my first day out
of hospital, then she left me, and after a time I thought
perhaps I would go to bed and I called her so that she could
take the tea-tray away. But there wasn't any answer and
when I went out to the kitchen she wasn't there, and she
wasn't in her bedroom upstairs either and nor was her suitcase
or any of her clothes. So I went to my room and sat down on
the bed and tried to think about what could have happened,
and then I suddenly noticed that one of the drawers of my
dressing-table was half open. It happened to be the drawer in
which I keep my jewel-case, and I went to take a look in it
and it was completely emptied out. Everything was gone, my
rings and my ear-rings and my necklaces and my brooches.
Nothing really valuable, you understand. I never had anything that was really valuable, but there were things Malcolm
had given me, and some I'd inherited from my mother and
things like that. Things I cared about, you know, though I

don't suppose they'd be worth more than three or four hundred pounds, if that. But they were all gone."

Her voice began to shake and I thought that in another moment she would be in tears.

"But this is serious," Felix said. "We must tell the police."

"No, oh no, don't do that!" she cried. "They wouldn't take any notice. They're busy with something else. Do you know what it is, Virginia? What are they all so busy with?"

Felix and I exchanged glances, each trying to induce the other to give some advice as to what would be best to tell this sick and excited old woman.

I decided that the truth might be as good as anything else.

"A horrible thing has happened next door," I said. "Someone got into the house, the police haven't told us how they think it was done, and he killed Mrs. Bulpitt. I think she was killed by a blow on the head, though the police haven't told us about that either."

"Murder!" Julia exclaimed.

"Yes," I said. "Murder."

"In Ellsworthy Street!" Her eyes had become round and staring. The threat of tears was gone, but it looked to me as if instead of them she might start screaming.

Felix spoke hastily. "I'll go and get hold of that man Dawnay and tell him about your jewellery. For all we know, it may be important."

"No, oh no!" she repeated. "It sounds so trivial now. Mrs. Bulpitt's dead, really dead?"

"Yes," I said.

"I never liked her, you know, but to think that she's dead . . . She got me that girl, didn't she?"

"Sue Lockett?"

"Yes."

"She did, as a matter of fact."

"I don't mean there's any connection, but it's interesting, isn't it? I mean, that she should have known a girl like that, a really bad sort of girl without any morals, and then get herself murdered? I wonder if Mrs. Bulpitt knew the kind of girl she was sending me. Do you think she did?"

"I'm sure she didn't," I said, though really I was impelled only by that fearful prohibition that one must not speak ill of the dead, for the very same question had begun to stir in my mind. I was thinking of the evening dresses and the shoes and the cosmetics and wondering what kind of person we had had living amongst us in Ellsworthy Street.

"If you'll forgive me, Mrs. Creed," Felix said, "I'm going to tell the police about your jewellery. It could be that there's some connection between that girl and Mrs. Bulpitt, and in that case they ought to be told about it."

She considered it, then shook her head. "I'd sooner you didn't. It would be different if the jewellery was valuable, but it isn't. It's just that I loved nearly every bit of it. And I'd better be getting home. Perhaps, Mr. Freer, you would see me across the street. Then the police can come and talk to me at home, if they want to."

"Oh, you're not going, Julia!" I said. "You can stay here the night. You can't go back to that empty house."

"Yes, dear, I think that would be best," she said, rising shakily to her feet. "Then I can show the police my empty jewel-case, if they're interested, and perhaps they'll take fingerprints of that girl. They must be all over the place. And there might be some of that young man too, who brought her and who's sure to know all about the theft, don't you think? In fact, he might be—let me see, what's the word for it?—a pimp. No, that's what prostitutes have, isn't it? But of course,

WOMAN SLAUGHTER 89

she may have been a prostitute. Isn't it terrible, once you get over the edge of the normal world you're used to, what fearful thoughts you have? People like that have never been real to me before."

She stooped to give Jinks one more pat, then walked slowly towards the door.

"I wish you'd stay, Julia," I said. "I could go over and fetch your night-clothes for you, and you could have the room where Felix has been sleeping and he could sleep on the sofa in here. And the police could come and talk to you here and one of us could let them into your house, if you'd give us the key, and they could investigate everything they want to."

"No, dear, it's sweet of you, but I think I'll go home. I never sleep well in a strange bed. But come over and see me tomorrow, if you've time. I'll look forward to that."

She and Felix went out together.

I sat there for some time, wondering what I ought to do. If only Julia had agreed to stay it would have made everything relatively simple. The thought of her spending the night alone in the house across the street worried me very much. Then it occurred to me that I had not really tried very hard to persuade her to stay and eat one of Felix's omelettes with us.

But perhaps that did not really matter. The chances were that she would have no appetite at all. And anyway, as Felix was seeing her home, he would probably have thought of this himself and would make her let him into the house to provide food for her and see her into bed. Whatever failings he might have had as a husband, he seldom forgot that people should have at least three meals a day, and he was always ready to provide them. If he had never had the mental persistence to qualify as a doctor, he might, if he had chosen, have become an excellent nurse.

When he had been gone a little while I got up and picked up the telephone directory, hunted through it, found the Gambrells' number, and dialled it.

A woman's voice answered me.

"Mrs. Gambrell?" I said.

"Speaking," she answered.

"This is Virginia Freer," I said. "If you remember, we met this morning at the Gleesons."

"Oh yes, of course," she said. "You're a friend of Mrs. Bulpitt's."

"I wonder if you can help me?" There had been something about the woman that morning that had irritated me, but I tried very hard not to let that sound in my voice now. "I believe you said you're on the committee of a group called Help in Need."

She gave a little laugh. "I am, as a matter of fact. My husband badgered me into doing it. He said it was the sort of thing that would be expected of a wife of his. But I'm not really that kind of person at all. I mean, I don't like committees and getting mixed up in all sorts of things. I'm really a rather solitary sort of person, not a 'joiner' of things, if you know what I mean. Of course I like to see my friends, my real friends, from time to time, but somehow I hardly know how to sit through those awful meetings, trying to talk to the sort of people one simply doesn't want to know."

I remembered her beautiful emerald green dress and thought that her real friends must be on the affluent side. I was probably one of those whom she would have no wish to know.

"Then perhaps you can't help me," I said.

"Oh dear, I didn't mean that," she said. "Is there really something I can do? Of course I'll help if there is, though it seems unlikely. What's the trouble?"

"Have you heard that Mrs. Bulpitt's dead?" I asked.

"But I thought you told me that it was some poor old man who'd been knocked down in your street?"

"That's correct," I said. "But it happens that since I saw you Mrs. Bulpitt has been murdered."

There was a silence, which was not surprising. I decided not to break it.

At last she said, "You did say murdered?"

"Yes."

"You're serious? You aren't—well, playing some sort of trick on me? It isn't a joke?"

"I'm serious."

"Oh, my God!"

There was another silence, and when she spoke again the tone of her voice had completely altered. All the lightness had gone out of it. It was abrupt and sombre.

"How did it happen? And why?"

"The police don't know much about it yet," I said. "But I happen to be the person who found the body and called the police. I believe she'd been knocked on the head by our old friend, the blunt instrument, sometime between twelve and two or thereabouts, but why is something nobody knows about yet."

"My dear, how awful for you—finding her, you said?" Her voice had recovered itself, making her questions sound as if I had just reported to her that I had been caught in a shower without an umbrella. "But how can I possibly help? I hardly knew the poor woman."

"It isn't really about her that I'm ringing up," I said,

"though I had to make sure you understood what had happened. The fact is, I've a friend, Mrs. Creed, who lives just across the street from me and who's only just come out of hospital. And it was her husband who was killed on Friday evening. So you understand she isn't really fit to be left alone. I can't do much myself because I've got to go to my job tomorrow, and unfortunately a girl whom Mrs. Bulpitt got hold of through Help in Need to look after Mrs. Creed has decamped, taking all Mrs. Creed's jewellery with her. So I thought you were someone who just might be able to help. Could you find someone through Help in Need who might be able to take the girl's place?"

"But what a gruesome story!" Mrs. Gambrell sounded quite cheerful again. "Really horrendous. Of course I'll do anything I can, but don't count on me, will you? I'll start telephoning around and see if I can come up with anything, but it's very short notice. You say this girl who made off with your friend's jewellery was sent to her by Mrs. Bulpitt?"

"Yes."

"It just shows, doesn't it? I mean, all these people who are up to the eyes in virtue and good causes simply don't know a bad egg when they see one. I'm most terribly sorry about everything, of course. Do the police think the girl had anything to do with Mrs. Bulpitt's murder?"

"I don't know if they even know yet about the girl going missing."

"Murder. You really mean murder? She wasn't just knocked out and is going to come to in hospital?"

"I'm afraid not."

"Was it a sex crime, do you know? You hear such awful things about women in their eighties being attacked by boys of sixteen and raped and strangled."

"The police haven't told me anything to suggest that," I said.

"Well, I'll see if I can do anything to help. I really feel for that poor friend of yours. I'll telephone later in the evening if I've been able to find anyone to help out. Only one feels nervous, doesn't one, taking the responsibility of sending along someone one really knows nothing about? As Mrs. Bulpitt must have done."

We both rang off. Only a few minutes later Felix came back into the house.

I thought that he would tell me what he had been able to do for Julia, and whether or not he had reported the theft of her jewellery to the police who were still going in and out of the house next door, but he threw himself down in a chair without speaking and frowned angrily into space. I wondered if something had happened while he was out to add to the distresses of the day and make him wish, even more than he probably had been doing already, that he had driven straight through Allingford and on to London, instead of stopping in Ellsworthy Street. He did not look in a mood to make omelettes.

"I'll get the supper," I said.

"Wait a minute," he said quickly, as I went towards the door. "Don't go yet. I've got to tell you something."

I stood still in the doorway.

"It's best that I should tell you before anyone else does," he said, turning his head to look at me. His eyes were as sad as those of poor Jinks. "You see, I killed Mrs. Bulpitt."

FIVE

I AM ACCUSTOMED to Felix's fantasies. At times I have even enjoyed them, so long as I have felt sure that he himself knew they were fantasies. On the occasions when I have felt that he was beginning to believe in them himself I have become frightened. But I have listened to him describing to a suitably credulous audience how he crossed the Greenland ice-cap alone on skis, and I have only been entertained by it. I have heard him tell and even be believed how once in Australia, having been separated from his party in the desert, rescued by some prowling Aborigines, and robbed of all his clothes so that he had to go naked for some weeks, he was kept alive by the natives on a diet of maggots. To the best of my knowledge he has never been out of this country, unless perhaps to Boulogne to buy some duty-free wine, but his stories can be astonishingly convincing, mainly because they have come out of books that he has read recently and has studied very thoughtfully. But I have never heard him describe himself as a murderer.

I came back into the room and sat down.

"Exactly what are you trying to say?" I asked.

"What I've said," he answered. "I killed Mrs. Bulpitt."

"You know that's nonsense."

He looked irritated. "You never believe anything I say."

"With reason."

"But this is true, Virginia. Dead true. I don't mean I hit her on the head myself, but it's perfectly possible to kill someone without being on the spot. And that's what I've done. I murdered her."

I shook my head. "No, something may have happened that you've somehow got yourself involved in, but murder isn't your line."

"I don't mean I *meant* to kill her," he said. "I didn't."

"Then at worst it's manslaughter."

"Call it woman-slaughter in this case."

"That seems appropriate. Now tell me what you've really got on your mind."

A new cigarette had to be lit before he could answer, and even after he had drawn smoke deeply into his lungs and sent it seeping out slowly through his nostrils, he only sat frowning at the glowing bars of the electric fire and did not reply. I thought that he was probably working out whether to tell me the truth or give me some colourful version of something not so far distant from it as to be incredible.

At last he said, "It goes back to that accident in the street out here when the old chap was killed. I haven't really told you the whole truth about it."

"You mean you saw more than you've admitted?" I said. Many years ago I had got past feeling surprised at anything that he might say.

"I'm afraid so," he said. "But I wasn't actually sure about it. Not by any means. It's just that as that Jaguar took off from in front of Mrs. Bulpitt's house I did notice the end of its number. Not the whole of it, just the end. It was VTF.

You remember what a foggy evening it was, and for some
reason I said to myself straight away, 'that stands for "Very
Thick Fog." ' And that amused me and I found the letters
very easy to remember, whereas I can never keep a series of
numbers in my head for more than a moment. I can't remember the telephone numbers even of the people I ring up most
often. But VTF stuck in my head, and then on Saturday
evening, when you were over at Mrs. Creed's and then at
Mrs. Bulpitt's, a very odd thing happened. I took Jinks for a
walk and we went quite a long way and we got into a square,
I think called Durkin Square, Georgian mostly, and nearly all
the houses had brass plates by their doors, and there in front
of one of them was a Jaguar and the last letters on its number-
plate were VTF."

"Durkin Square," I said. "That's where most of our medicals have their consulting rooms, and a good many of them
live there. But if you'd looked round I expect you'd have
seen another two or three Jaguars."

"I did look round and there wasn't one," he replied. "A
Rolls or two, but no Jaguars. And even if there had been any,
how many of them do you think would have had VTF on
their number-plates?"

"So what did you do about it?"

"I stood and pondered. Actually I stood there for quite a
while. I didn't want to do anything rash. Then I went up the
steps, to the front door of the house in front of which the car
was standing, and had a look at the name on the brass plate
beside the door. It was Denis Gambrell. It was—"

"Gambrell!" I interrupted him. "Are you sure of that?
Gambrell?"

"Oh yes, and all the usual letters after his name, of course.
Why?"

"Only that I met a Dr. Gambrell and his wife at the Gleesons' party this morning, and he certainly didn't strike me as the sort of man who'd be driving around the town drunk and knocking people down and not stopping. Are you sure you went to the right house, Felix?"

"Actually I wasn't dead sure about it at the time, but now I am."

"I don't understand."

"It's quite simple really. You see, I began by thinking that the car might have been parked in front of that particular house more or less by chance. What I mean is, the cars there were pretty well nose-to-tail all the way round the square. Naturally none of those old houses have garages and someone might just have put his car into an empty space he happened to see. So I decided I ought to check. There's a phone box in the square and I got Gambrell's number from Directory Inquiries and then . . ." He threw his half-smoked cigarette away into the empty grate with a gesture of violence that was not characteristic of him. "Then I did something I ought never to have done. Something bloody stupid, and as it's turned out, bloody dangerous. But at the time I was really only curious."

"Yes, yes, but what was it?" I asked.

"I rang up Gambrell," he answered, "just dialled the number and waited. And after a moment a man's voice said 'Yes?' And I said—I swear to you, Virginia, it was all I said— 'Ellsworthy Street.' And there was dead silence. Then the phone his end was put down and that was that. I put mine down too and came away. But you see what it means, don't you?"

"I'm not sure that I do." When Felix starts swearing to the truth of what he is saying I always feel very dubious. All the same, I felt an unpleasant tingling down my spine, as if I had taken in more than I realised.

"Well, you see, until that happened I'd been saying to myself that someone perhaps could have pinched his car and gone joy-riding in it and been responsible for the accident, or that the letters on the number-plate could have been coincidence and I'd got the wrong car. But when he reacted like that it was obvious that those mere words, 'Ellsworthy Street,' meant something special to him. That's why he said nothing and then rang off. He was dead scared."

"He may have thought he was just being bothered by some crank."

"But what is there about those two words to suggest a crank? Don't you think, if that's what he thought, he'd probably have asked, 'Who's speaking?' or something like that? So I came away saying to myself, 'My dear Dr. Gambrell, I think you were probably driving that car last night that killed Mr. Creed, and sooner or later I expect you're going to have to pay for it.' Of course, I hadn't met him, as you have, so I didn't know if he was the kind of person who'd do that sort of thing. Not that I'm all that convinced by your intuitions about him. Some people change their personalities entirely when they get drunk, and I don't suppose he was drunk at your party. But it's said that lots of medicals take to drink, from the sheer strain of their jobs, or drugs even. However, the plain fact is that when I said 'Ellsworthy Street' he was shocked and frightened. And you've got to remember what happened this morning."

"That thousand pounds to Mrs. Bulpitt," I said, beginning to feel that I knew what was coming.

"Exactly," he said. "That thousand pounds. Delivered to Mrs. Bulpitt the morning after I made that telephone call.

Paid to keep her quiet because he'd visited her for some reason and he believed she would put pressure on him about the accident afterwards."

"Blackmail. He believed that she was going to blackmail him."

"Yes."

"But Felix, you haven't told me the whole story about that telephone call of yours, have you?"

"I have. Really I have."

"No, because it was on Saturday evening that you suddenly asked me to define blackmail. It was already on your mind before you knew anything about the thousand pounds."

"And you said it was extorting money with menaces."

"But why did you want that definition that evening?"

"Just coincidence. It's an interesting subject."

"Felix, do remember that you're talking to Virginia!" I said. "We know each other rather well, don't we? Of course you said more than just 'Ellsworthy Street' to Dr. Gambrell."

"Nothing of any significance, I do assure you."

"But something."

"Well, perhaps my memory isn't absolutely clear on the subject. Perhaps after saying 'Ellsworthy Street' I said something like, 'People like you should pay for what they've done.' As I told you, I know I said something of the sort to myself, but perhaps I said it to him too, and if so it may have sounded as if I was going to blackmail him. But I'm quite sure I didn't menace him and I didn't try to extort money, so it couldn't possibly be construed as blackmail, could it?"

"There's one thing you still haven't explained," I said.

"What's that?"

"Why did he send the money to Mrs. Bulpitt? Her voice on the telephone, whether he actually recognized it or not,

would have been a woman's. Yours is a man's. Why should
he think you were ringing up for her?"

"There could be all sorts of reasons for that. He may have
known she had a connection with some man. For instance,
what about the man you saw coming out of her house on the
way home from your party?"

I nodded. "Yes, it's possible. But now you're blaming
yourself for having caused her death."

For a little while he looked blank, as if he could not think
what I was talking about. Then he said abruptly, "Yes."

"You believe that Dr. Gambrell was the driver of the car
you saw here on Friday evening," I said, "and that he thought
when you telephoned him that Mrs. Bulpitt was starting
blackmail, and that he came here today, sometime after having been at the Gleesons' party, and killed her. And you're
responsible for that because of that telephone call."

"Isn't it obvious?"

"That he's the murderer of Mrs. Bulpitt?"

"Yes, that, of course. But it was my call that put it into his
head."

"If you're so sure of it, why haven't you told the police
about it?"

"I can't say I'm absolutely *sure,* you know. It's hard
enough to be sure of anything ever, and in a case of this sort
one ought to be particularly careful not to accuse some perfectly innocent person of something they've never even
thought of doing."

"But listen, Felix, and please take this seriously, you really
did make that telephone call yesterday evening, did you? It
isn't imaginary?"

"I swear to you, Virginia—"

"Don't!" I interrupted him. "Forget I asked the question.

But at least you did see a Jaguar with VTF on the number-plate outside Dr. Gambrell's house."

"I did."

"But he and his wife didn't come to the Gleesons' party in a Jaguar. There were several cars outside their house when I left, and if there'd been a Jaguar I'd have noticed it. But the only cars there were a fairly ordinary collection."

"The Gambrells have probably got a second car, and perhaps a third and a fourth. Personally I think the number of cars a family owns should be rationed. The motor car is killing itself. The time's coming when people will have to prove that they have any serious need to own a car at all, or Britain will become one long traffic jam from north to south and we'll think of parking as some picturesque old thing, that people did in days long gone by."

His voice had been becoming earnestly excited. This was a subject on which he felt deeply and sincerely. It happened that the last time he had stayed with me he had had one leg in plaster; it had been broken by his having been run into by a boy riding his bicycle on the pavement. Though Felix had at one time made a living of a sort by selling very unreliable second-hand cars, and still drove a car himself, bicycles, motorcycles, cars, vans, lorries—indeed anything that moved on wheels and belonged to anyone but himself—filled him almost with hatred. This excluded trains, for which he had a good deal of affection.

Thinking that as he had now started to brood on his phobia, and that for the moment this would keep his mind off murder, I decided to go out to the kitchen and make the mushroom omelettes, in the concoction of which he had been interrupted by Julia Creed's visit.

My omelettes were probably not as good as his would have

been, but with some bread and butter to go with them, followed by cheese, they made an adequate supper, over which we hardly spoke. I was trying to make up my mind how much I believed of what he had told me, and, supposing that it was all more or less true, what I ought to do about it. If he would not tell the police what had happened, ought I to do it myself? He could then either confirm or deny it, but at least would not be able merely to suppress it for no other reason than that he intensely disliked talking about anything to the police.

His face was unusually unexpressive while we ate. I wondered if he had begun to repent having told me as much as he had. It put him to some extent in my power, and feeling himself to be in the power of anyone else always brought out the worst in him. I had never noticed that he enjoyed the feeling of having power over some other person, but that anyone should have power over him was something that he found unendurable, and he was likely to take some kind of revenge for it.

It was after we had finished our meal and I had set the dishwasher going that the front doorbell rang again. This time it really was the police. Detective Superintendent Dawnay and Sergeant Wells were on the doorstep, and with an apology from the superintendent for disturbing me yet again that evening, they came straight into the house, almost before I had time to invite them in. I took them into the sitting-room. Felix was not there and I thought at first that he intended to avoid meeting the two men, but then he came in, greeted them casually, and went to stand by the window, somehow expressing by his attitude that he did not expect them to stay for long.

That meant, I concluded, that he had no intention of tell-

ing them what he had told me about recognizing the Jaguar
or about his telephone call to Dr. Gambrell. And that left me
worrying, as I had been while we ate our omelettes, about
whether or not I should tell them the story myself. If I had
had more faith than I did in what Felix had told me I suppose
I would have told them everything immediately, but as it was
I waited politely for them to tell me why they had come.

They both sat down side by side on the sofa, and I sat in a
chair facing them.

Dawnay began in a soft yet challenging tone, looking me
thoughtfully in the face. The eyes that looked so pale in his
dark face were both friendly and sardonic.

"That thousand pounds, Mrs. Freer," he said.

"Yes?" I said.

"You're absolutely sure of it, are you? You saw it come.
You saw Mrs. Bulpitt count it. It was a thousand pounds."

"Yes," I said again.

"And a young man brought it. He was wearing a helmet,
so you can't describe him. There was no address on the wrapping, or any explanation inside of why it had been sent."

"That's what I told you earlier today," I said.

"And you're quite sure of all of it? You don't want to alter
anything?"

His friendly tone was beginning to annoy me, because his
eyes were so sceptical. I felt as if he were accusing me of
something, though I could not think of what.

"I'm absolutely sure," I said.

"It's only that we've searched that house from top to bot-
tom and we haven't found any thousand pounds. Of course
we'll go on searching. We may have missed some special
hiding-place she had. But so far we've found nothing but a
handbag in her bedroom, in which there was about fifty

pounds in five-pound notes and some loose change. It looks as
if that's where she kept her money for running expenses. But
there's no sign of that thousand pounds."

"Then probably the murderer took it," I said. "It might
even have been the motive for the murder."

"That's possible, of course," he agreed. "But I believe you
said she took the money out of the room and you don't know
where she put it."

"All she told me was that she was going to put it in a safe
place," I said. "I don't know where that was."

"Yet if getting hold of it was the motive for the murder,"
he said, "the murderer must have known where it was to be
found. That's if the crime was premeditated. But perhaps Mrs.
Bulpitt didn't put it in a safe place at all, but just put it down
somewhere where the murderer happened to see it and he
helped himself to it after he had killed her. Money always
comes in useful."

"Is that what you think?" I asked.

"What do you think yourself?"

Before I had time to answer, Felix had turned and walked
a couple of paces into the room.

"What about the wrapping paper?" he asked. "Have you
found that?"

"I wondered if you'd ask that," the superintendent said.
"No, we haven't found it."

"So you aren't sure if there ever was any thousand
pounds," I said, my resentment beginning to boil. "You think
that for some mysterious reason of my own I made it up."

He shook his head. "No, I think I believe in it."

"Then why are you asking me all these questions?"

He thrust his hand through his dark hair. For someone as

lightly built as he was his hands looked very broad and powerful.

"Stealing the money and removing the wrapping paper as well gives us a rather curious picture, doesn't it?" he said. "It suggests the murderer may have known the money came in a package. If he had just picked up a wad of bank notes that he happened to see lying about, why should he think of looking for some wrapping paper they'd come in? But if he knew they'd come in a package he might have been afraid that it could somehow lead to his identification. Tell me, Mrs. Freer, the young man in the helmet whom you saw deliver the package, can you tell me whether or not he was wearing gloves?"

I thought about it. I tried to recall what I had seen through the window. Then I shook my head.

"I'm sorry," I said, "I didn't notice."

He did not press me. He and the sergeant exchanged glances and seemed to agree about something, then Dawnay said, "Something that might interest you. We've identified the man you saw coming out of Mrs. Bulpitt's house when you were driving home from your party."

"How did that happen?" I asked.

"He came to us. He heard about the murder on the six o'clock news and came to us at once. He's Mrs. Bulpitt's nephew, or that at least is what he claims to be."

The way that he put it puzzled me.

"Have you any reason to doubt it?"

"No, but no proof of it either. But his photograph is on her mantelpiece and it happens that there's a copy of her will in the same bureau where she kept her bank statements and her share certificates. The original will is with a solicitor in

London. And in this will it appears that she left everything
she had to him."

"What's his name?"

"Hamlyn. Godfrey Hamlyn." He paused. "You're sure
you've never heard her talk about him?"

"Quite sure. I didn't even know she had a nephew."

"She seems to have been a very reticent lady."

It had never struck me before that she had been. I had
never thought about her background any more than I had
about that of most of my neighbours. It would never have
seemed natural to me to question them about their families
and their pasts if they did not choose of themselves to talk
about them. And if they did I would probably have felt no
more than a moderate amount of interest.

"What was he doing here?" I asked.

"Just visiting his aunt, so he said," Dawnay answered.

"He doesn't live in Allingford, does he?"

"No, in London. But he's staying here for the present. He's
a photographer by profession. That picture of him on the
mantelpiece was a self-portrait, he said. He expresses great
shock at his aunt's death, but it would appear that he stands to
gain a good deal by it. Not that that's against him. More
murders are committed for entirely irrational reasons than for
simple cold-blooded matters of gain." He turned again to the
sergeant. "Those photographs, Wells," he said. "I'd like Mrs.
Freer to look at them."

The sergeant had been carrying a briefcase. He opened it
and extracted something in a plastic envelope. He handed this
to Dawnay, who took from it what turned out to be two
photographs, and held them out to me.

"Don't worry," he said, "they've been tested for fingerprints. The only ones on them are Mrs. Bulpitt's and this man

Hamlyn's. And there were some duplicates in her drawer. But I'd like to know if you recognize either of the ladies."

I took the photographs from him and as I did so Felix came to stand behind me so that he could look at them over my shoulder. They were both coloured. One was of a very slender woman with auburn hair, wearing a close-fitting dress of broad black and white stripes, with a big black bow on her hip and the skirt slit from hem to hip, showing a very shapely thigh. The bosom was cut so deeply that her nipples were only just concealed. The other photograph was of a girl of much more solid build, with heavy features in a long, narrow face and dark brown hair tied back in a pony-tail. She was wearing the most exiguous of bikinis.

"Do you recognize them?" the superintendent asked.

"Yes, I do," I said. "This one . . ." I held out the one of the woman in the black and white dress, ". . . is Mrs. Gambrell, the wife of Dr. Gambrell, who's a consultant gynaecologist at St. Mary's Hospital. This one . . ." I held out the other, ". . . is a girl called Sue Lockett. I believe I told you she's been working for an association called Help in Need, who send out people to do the housekeeping for you and generally look after you when you've been ill, and that sort of thing. Mrs. Bulpitt was on their committee. And she was responsible for sending this girl, Sue Lockett, to work for Mrs. Creed, whose husband was killed in an accident in the road here on Friday, and who'd been in hospital, having an operation, and only came home this morning. And that reminds me . . ." I hesitated and looked up at Felix.

"Yes," he said. "Go on."

"Well, Mrs. Creed came over here earlier this evening," I said. "She shouldn't have done it. She isn't fit to be out. But she came because she wanted to tell us about a rather horrid

thing that had happened. She and this girl hadn't been getting
on at all well, and then Sue disappeared and with her all Mrs.
Creed's jewellery. My husband and I tried to persuade her to
tell you about it at once, but when she heard what had happened to Mrs. Bulpitt she said none of the jewellery was
valuable and that it was all too trivial to bother you about
when you'd something so much more important on your
hands. But I don't know anything about the girl, I mean,
where she lived or where she came from. Mrs. Bulpitt told
me they'd had good reports of her from other jobs she'd been
in. Oh—" I paused because suddenly something that I had
forgotten had just come back to me. "She's got a boy-friend.
He's a boy called Simon Prescott and he brought Sue to the
house. And he's got a black eye."

It worried me that neither of the detectives looked particularly surprised at anything that I had said. Not nearly as
surprised as I felt myself. I concluded that they probably
knew most of it already and for reasons best known to themselves were testing me in some way.

I began to want to tell them more, to see whether I could
surprise them if I really tried. I wanted to tell them about
Felix having recognized the Jaguar in Durkin Square and
having telephoned Dr. Gambrell. But Felix himself was silent
on the subject. He had put a hand on to my shoulder and was
digging his fingers into it, which I took to be a warning to
me not to talk. Realising that if I did I might get him into
trouble, I sat waiting to see if the detectives had anything
more to say.

Evidently they had not, for they both stood up and
Dawnay thanked me for having been so helpful. They were
just leaving when Felix said, "That man Hamlyn, d'you
know where he's staying?"

"He gave the Rose and Crown as his address for the present," the superintendent replied. The Rose and Crown was an old pub that had been converted into the best hotel in Allingford. "Naturally he's also given us his London address. But if I may give you a piece of advice, Mr. Freer, don't try to get mixed up in this. Leave the man alone. Murder is a job for professionals."

Felix looked offended. "Did I suggest I wanted to get mixed up in it? The truth is, the last thing I want is to get involved. My presence here is quite coincidental."

"I'm glad to hear it. Well, good evening."

The two men made for the front door.

When they had gone I returned to the sitting-room, dropped into a chair, and closed my eyes. My head was throbbing.

"Oh God, I'm tired," I said. "I don't remember ever feeling so tired."

"Then go to bed," Felix advised.

"Those photographs," I said, "they knew whom they were of, didn't they?"

"That was my impression."

"I wonder what they wanted from me."

"Just wanting to see whether or not you'd seen them before. I suppose you hadn't?"

"Certainly not. And I find it very interesting that Mrs. Bulpitt had that photograph of Mrs. Gambrell. I wonder what she was before she married the good doctor. On the stage, do you think?"

"Quite likely. Now really I'd go to bed, Virginia. You do look terribly tired."

"I suppose you're going to visit the Rose and Crown."

"I might."

"Well, good night," I said.

"Good night."

We kissed each other very lightly and I went upstairs to bed. I fell asleep so soon that I did not know when Felix also went to bed.

I had to get up fairly early next day as it was one of my mornings at the clinic. Sandra Baker arrived to work for me, and as usual she and Louella came before I was ready to set out. She was likely, I thought, to want a good gossip about what had happened next door, and I should have to cut it short if I wanted to be in time for my first appointment. But what she said as she extricated the vacuum cleaner from the cupboard where it was kept had nothing to do with the murder.

"My Jim got his jaw bashed last night," she said.

Louella, who normally followed at her mother's heels, looked astonished.

"Mum, you never said!" she protested.

"Well, he did," Sandra said. "At that pub down the road, the Red Lion. Some kids got into a fight in the bar and instead of dealing with it themselves, sensible-like, they sent for the police and Jim was sent along. And that young Prescott, who's always getting into trouble, took a swing at him and bashed him. That boy's going to get into real trouble before long, I shouldn't wonder."

"Prescott?" I said. "Simon Prescott?"

"That's him."

"Mum, why didn't Dad bash the other man?" Louella asked.

Sandra gave a grin. "Who said he didn't?"

"Did this Simon Prescott get arrested?" I inquired.

"No." Sandra spoke with derision. "Jim got them sorted

out. There's enough serious trouble about without making a
fuss about a thing like that. There's all this trouble next door,
for instance. Jim always tells me everything, which maybe he
shouldn't, I don't know, but it seems sort of natural to talk
about what's been happening, and he's told me a lot about
Mrs. Bulpitt. Not that he's in on the case, him only being a
constable, but it seems they've been keeping an eye on her
ever since she came to live here, her having been inside, you
see, and perhaps having ideas of getting up to her old tricks."

"Inside?" I said. "Do you mean in prison?"

"That's right. It wasn't for long, but she did a stretch, and
it was only after she came out that she came to settle here."

"But why on earth should Mrs. Bulpitt have been in
prison?"

"Ah, that's kind of interesting," Sandra said. "Seems she
used to be a madam, you know what I mean, ran a brothel or
something of that sort and did very well out of it, I believe,
but in the end got in bad trouble and had to pay for it. It's
kind of funny, isn't it, when you think of her as she was here,
always so badly dressed and sitting on charitable committees
and all? I know I didn't ought, but I can't help laughing."

"Sandra," I said, "how long have you known all this about
her?"

She was trailing the vacuum cleaner into the sitting-room.
I followed her. Felix had joined us while she had been talking
and remained in the doorway, listening.

"Only since yesterday," she answered. "Jim had this fight
in the pub and when he got home he wanted a drink, and
then another, and that got him talking all about the murder
next door and he told me, like I said, how they'd been keeping an eye on Mrs. Bulpitt ever since she came here. But she
seemed to have retired. They never found out anything

against her. But of course, with a past like that, almost anyone might have murdered her. I mean, any of all those people
she had photographs of, if she was inclined to make use of
them."

"Photographs," I said. "She had a photograph of Mrs.
Gambrell and a girl called Sue Lockett, who was supposed to
be helping Mrs. Creed and then went off with her jewellery."

Sandra gave a hoot of laughter. "Is that what they showed
you, just Mrs. Gambrell and the Lockett girl?"

"Yes," I said. "Were there others?"

"Heaps of them, so Jim said. And if those were the only
ones they showed you, it may have been because they were
the only ones they felt they could show a lady like you. Jim
told me about them, said he'd have liked to keep two or three
himself. 'Now don't you talk like that,' I said, 'you're not
having anything like that in my house.' Of course he was
only joking, but he told me about them, real porn he said
they were, enough to make even him kind of embarrassed,
and in his job you've got to get used to most things."

"This is very interesting," Felix said. "From running a
brothel to running Help in Need—is the gap really so enor-
mous? They supply a rather different kind of service, but both
involve the organizing of a number of women. Allow that
she'd had a change of heart while she was in prison and had
changed her mind about what she could give to society, you
might say there's a kind of similarity about the two jobs. This
girl, Sue Lockett, I wonder which part of Mrs. Bulpitt's life
she was really connected with."

Sandra looked at him blankly, not certain how far he expected her to take him seriously. After a moment she decided
to titter.

"I'll tell Jim that," she said. "He'll enjoy it. He's got a great sense of humour."

"There's just something I'd like to know," Felix said. "The two photographs that man Dawnay showed us were, as you've heard, perfectly proper. A bit surprising, because one wouldn't have expected Mrs. Bulpitt to have any photograph at all of Mrs. Gambrell, let alone one like that. But did he choose them to show to my wife only because they were the most decent? It surprises me somehow that the police should be so sensitive, though perhaps I'm doing them a wrong. All the same, was there another reason? I'm wondering if it happened that they were the only ones of people who are known to live here in Allingford?"

Sandra wrinkled her forehead in uncertainty. "You mean all the others could have come from London or somewhere?"

"That's what I was thinking," he said.

"I don't know. I'll ask Jim. He'll know all about it. They all talk about these things down at the station more than they ought when it's something interesting. Now I'd better get on with my work."

She plugged in the vacuum cleaner, pressed the switch on it, and it began to hum. I took the money I owed her out of my handbag and told her that I would leave it in the kitchen, then, knowing that I would be late for my appointment at the clinic, hurried out to the garage.

I had a busy day and it was late afternoon before I returned home. I found Felix, as was to be expected, lying on the sofa, smoking a cigarette and gazing at the ceiling. I have never known anyone with such a gift for idleness as he has. What passes through his mind while he spends time in this way I have never been able to fathom. At one time I had thought that some poem might emerge from all this abstraction, or some philosophical speculation, but in the end I came to the conclusion that he simply enjoyed thinking about nothing.

Because Sandra had been there that morning the fire had been laid, and now was alight, making the room look cheerful. Even Felix, for the moment, seemed to fit into the homely atmosphere.

"Where's Jinks?" I asked.

"Ah, there I think I've done something rather clever," he said. "You didn't really want to keep him, did you? A dog's almost as much of a tie as a baby."

"You've taken him back to Julia, have you?" I said. I thought of her saying that Jinks would have to be put down and I shrank from the thought. I did not honestly want to have to look after a dog, but I could not face the probability that the poor old creature would be killed.

"Oh no," Felix said, "it was much simpler than that. I simply asked that child Louella if she would like a dog, and of course she immediately started shrieking that she'd got to have him. Her mother tried to prevent it, but she hadn't a chance. Louella flung her arms round Jinks and declared she'd die if she couldn't have him. So your Sandra departed presently with child plus dog."

"And you may have lost me Sandra's services," I said. "If she's annoyed enough about it she may blame me and never come again, and if that doesn't worry you much you may regret the fact that we won't hear any more of Jim's experiences."

"No, on the whole she took it quite well," Felix said. "In the end I think I talked her into the idea that a child ought to have a pet, which I think is perfectly true, and she realised she was getting one for free."

"But I ought to go over and tell Julia what we've done

about him," I said, "and see how she's getting on. It's a pity it's been one of my busy days. I'd have looked in on her long ago if I could have got away."

"She's all right," Felix said. "I went over myself about one o'clock. I thought it might help if I made her some lunch. But she'd got help there already and I didn't stay."

"Help?" I said. "Has one of the other neighbours rallied round?"

"Not a neighbour exactly," Felix answered. "And I didn't stay to inquire how she happened to be there. But I recognized her at once from the photograph we saw. It was the wife of that eminent consultant at St. Mary's Hospital, Dr. Gambrell."

SIX

WHEN I RANG Julia Creed's doorbell it was Mrs. Gambrell who opened the door to me. I put as much surprise into my voice as I could and exclaimed, "Mrs. Gambrell!"

In a way, of course, I was very surprised to see her there, even though Felix had warned me of it.

"Call me Harriet," she said in a tone of extreme weariness. She was wearing well-cut black slacks and a cleverly knitted black and white sweater. It seemed to be a colour scheme that she especially favoured. It certainly went well with her auburn hair. But her face was very tired. "You've come to see Mrs. Creed, of course. I think she's doing quite well. She got dressed and she's been downstairs most of the day. But a little while ago she went upstairs to lie down. I promised to take her up some sherry presently."

"But what are you doing here?" I asked as I entered the house and she closed the front door behind me.

"When you rang up I did some telephoning around to see if I could find anyone to come in," she said, "but there didn't seem to be anyone available, so I thought I'd better come myself."

"That was very good of you."

She shrugged her shoulders. "I prefer it to sitting on committees. One at least sees results for oneself."

"If you want to go home I'll take over," I said. "I haven't got to go to work tomorrow."

"It's all right, I can stay," she said. "To tell the truth, I'm quite glad to be away from home at the moment. I expect you can guess why."

We were still standing in the hall at the foot of the stairs. I might have gone straight up them to see Julia, but it seemed to me that Harriet Gambrell was inclined to talk to me and I certainly felt inclined to talk to her.

"Do you mean because of some photographs the police showed me?" I asked.

"So they did show them to you. I wasn't sure."

"Yes, there was one of you and one of the girl called Sue Lockett, who came in to work for Julia."

She turned and led the way into the sitting-room, plainly expecting me to follow her. When I did, we both sat down and she stretched herself out in her chair, leaning her head against the back of it.

"It was such a shock, seeing the bloody thing after all this time, I had no sleep last night," she said. "It's been hard to keep going today."

"Then did the police come round to your home with it last night?" I asked.

"Yes, and of course showed it to my husband, to see how he reacted." She gave a hard little laugh. "I think he disappointed them. He said that it had been seeing the photograph that had first attracted him to me and asked them if they didn't think it was very attractive themselves. But of course that wasn't true. He'd never seen it before, and we had to have it out after they'd gone."

"But there was nothing so terrible about it," I said. "In fact, I should say it really was very attractive. I'd be happy if a photographer could produce anything as good of me."

She gave me an amused look, as if she did not think that that was likely to happen, in which she was right.

"Denis has always been afraid that my past might come to light," she said. "It was that that worried him, the fact that the police had somehow got hold of the photograph, not the thing itself."

"But you know how they got hold of it, don't you?" I said.

"Oh yes, they found it in old Ma Bulpitt's house," she said, "along with a lot of much less presentable things, or so I imagine, because she liked to keep lots of photographs that might sometime come in useful. She'd a nephew who was a photographer and he did the jobs for her without her victims knowing."

"Is it true then that she ran a brothel?" I asked.

She gave another laugh, harsh and brief. "You seem to have found out a lot during the last day or two. Did that man Dawnay actually tell you that?"

"No, as a matter of fact, he didn't. But I've got my sources, which I don't suppose I ought to reveal any more than if I was a journalist. It is true, is it?"

"I suppose you could call it that," she said with a sigh, "though she herself would probably have had a nicer name for it. She'd have said she liked to give parties, or something of that sort. I don't think she ever had exactly a resident staff. But I did meet my husband there, and Denis has always been afraid of the story getting out because he thought it might damage his position in the town, but she couldn't put the bite on us because if she'd tried that she'd have known we could turn her in, and she'd already been in prison before she decided to retire."

"You said she couldn't put the bite on you," I said, "but there's a problem of a thousand pounds that she was paid."

"A thousand pounds?" she said. "What does that mean?"

"I don't know," I said. "I don't know if it means anything."

"You didn't by any chance pay her a thousand pounds yourself, did you? She hadn't got anything on you?"

"No, I've never actually had to pay blackmail to anybody."

"I rather thought not." She looked as if she would have had a higher opinion of me if I had. "What's this about a thousand pounds?"

"Someone paid it to her," I said. "I saw it arrive and I saw her count it. She didn't seem to know who might have sent it. And according to the police, it's disappeared. They haven't been able to find it in the house. I believe they think it may have been picked up by the murderer."

"Then it's lucky for me I haven't got it. And didn't pay it. But unluckily I haven't an alibi for the time of the murder. Dawnay said they thought old Bulpitt was killed between twelve o'clock and two o'clock, and as you know, Denis and I were at that party of the Gleesons' from around twelve o'clock till about half past one, when most of the people left. Then I went home to lunch while Denis went to St. Mary's, I'm not sure why, but I suppose they could tell you, and so . . ." She paused. "Yes, I suppose they could tell you, but it's just possible . . . No!" She sat upright in her chair. "You're too damned easy to talk to. There was I, almost saying that perhaps Denis hasn't got an alibi any more than I have. That's nonsense, of course he has. I think he said he was going to have lunch with some doctor or other. Anyway, he'll have told the police about it. But you don't seem surprised at anything one says. It's a kind of relief, talking to you, because you seem to take everything one says for granted, but you're dangerous."

"I don't see how I can be if you've nothing to be afraid of." I did not explain to her how even the short years of my marriage to Felix had cured me of feeling very much surprise at the actions or statements of anybody. I had never made up my mind if this was a strength or a weakness. "How does it strike you, is a thousand pounds much or little to pay as blackmail?"

"I should think it all depends on who you are and what you've got to lose if your sins find you out, doesn't it?" she said. "If you're in the Cabinet, say, of course it's chicken feed. For people like us I'd call it a moderate sum. For a girl like Sue Lockett it would probably be the very limit of what she could pay."

"Sue Lockett?" I said. "Why has she suddenly come into it?"

"Oh, it was just a thought I had. I thought her reason for coming to work here might have been that the Bulpitt put pressure on her to do it. She's obviously got something on her or she wouldn't have bothered to keep her photograph, and she might have let her off some payment if the girl would look after Mrs. Creed. Managing to supply someone to help her neighbour was good for the Bulpitt image. But then the girl thought she'd escape from her clutches, grabbed Mrs. Creed's jewellery, and made off. She's probably in London by now."

It seemed likely enough to me.

"With or without the boy-friend, I wonder," I said.

"Oh, had she a boy-friend?"

"Yes, a boy called Simon Prescott, with a tendency to get into fights in pubs when he's had a few drinks. When I saw him he had a black eye and Sue told me he'd got it in a brawl in a pub, and last night he got in another one with our constable, Jim Baker, who got his jaw bashed. I heard it from Jim's wife this morning. And I've been thinking, ever since I met Prescott here, that he could have been the young man who delivered the thousand pounds to Mrs. Bulpitt. They both wore jeans and leather jackets, and though the one who delivered the money wore a helmet so that I couldn't recognize him, and he rode away on a motorbike, whereas Sue's friend drove off in a car, they were both about the same build and my impression is about the same age. And now you've made the suggestion that Sue could have been paying Mrs. Bulpitt blackmail, it strikes me it was quite likely he who brought her that mysterious money."

I had been so absorbed in what I was saying that I had not noticed how Harriet Gambrell's expression had altered, and not only her expression but the way in which she was holding her whole body. It had become rigid, with her hands clenched in her lap. She had opened her eyes very wide and was staring at me as if I were something that she would like to be able to crush underfoot. Her face had become very pale.

"I was talking nonsense," she said. "That girl couldn't have paid a thousand pounds to anyone. I expect she only came to oblige Mrs. Bulpitt. I expect Mrs. Bulpitt had been good to her in her time. She could be kind and generous occasionally."

"Not forgetting how the girl helped herself to the jewellery."

"Well, that was probably just a temptation that was too much for her. I've known other people like that."

So had I. There was one of them just across the street, except that Felix never pocketed the belongings of friends or of people who had put him in a position of trust.

"Suppose I go up and see Julia now," I said.

I thought that she looked relieved. "Yes, she'll be very glad to see you."

I found Julia lying on her bed, fully dressed except for her shoes, and reading a book. She did look pleased to see me.

"Isn't it a queer thing," she said, "I can't really manage to read? I've often thought in the past that I'd love to have a week of lying down, having someone to look after me, and have nothing to do but read. And now that I can do just that I can't keep my mind on what I'm reading for more than a few minutes. It may be after-effects of the anaesthetic or something. I'm just plain stupid. But how lucky I am to have Harriet here. She told me it was you who asked her to come. Thank you, dear, it was very thoughtful of you."

"I didn't exactly ask her to come," I said. "I asked her if she could find someone to help you, and it was her own idea to come herself."

"Was it really? She didn't tell me that. Then she's even nicer than I thought. She's been so good to me, much kinder than that awful girl who disappeared. But I feel I'm a bit of a fraud. I could perfectly well look after myself, you know. There's plenty of food in the freezer and all I'd have to do is heat it up, and Mrs. Bell, my daily, will be coming in as usual to clean in another couple of days. It doesn't come naturally to me, being dependent on other people."

"I shouldn't worry about that," I said. "Mrs. Gambrell told me she was glad to be away from home for the moment."

"Did she really? I wonder why that is."

"Don't most people feel it from time to time? I'd rather like to be away myself, staying in a luxurious hotel on some nice island away from our foul November climate." I had said more than I intended about Harriet Gambrell's desire to escape for a time from her home, and did my best to cover it up. "Now is there anything I can do for you? I'll be at home tomorrow and can do any shopping you'd like."

"I don't think there's anything we need at the moment, thank you, dear, but I'll telephone if I think of anything. There's just one thing . . ."

"Yes?"

"About Jinks. Are you really looking after him for me?"

"As a matter of fact, he's being looked after by my help, who's got a little girl who's fallen in love with him. If you'd like them to keep him, I think they will."

"That's good, that's very good. And there's one other thing. I don't know when the funeral's going to be. There's got to be an inquest first, I've been told. Isn't that terrible? I mean, when you're our age, like Malcolm and me, why can't death come peacefully, without any inquest and policemen coming and going, though I must say, they've been very considerate. But when the funeral happens, will you go with me? I'm ashamed to confess it, but I'm frightened of going alone. We've no children, you see, or even nephews or nieces, so I'd be glad to have someone I know to—well, to hold on to, if you know what I mean."

"Of course I'll go with you," I said. "Telephone as soon as you know when it's going to be and I'll make sure I can go."

Tears had come into her eyes and begun to trickle down her cheeks. She took no notice of them but only thanked me again. I gave her a kiss on her forehead and left her clutching

the book she could not read as if it helped her to hold on to
it.

When I reached home I told Felix as much as I could
remember of my talk with Harriet Gambrell.

Instead of commenting on it, Felix said, "How would you
like to go out to dinner?"

"To the Rose and Crown?" I said.

"That's what I was thinking of."

"Which just happens by chance to be the place where Mrs.
Bulpitt's nephew is staying."

"So it is."

"Well, I never mind being taken to dinner at the Rose and
Crown. Or am I taking you?" I never went out for a meal
with Felix without making sure that I had enough money
with me to pay for us both, in case it turned out that just
accidentally he had left his wallet at home.

"No, no, this is on me," he said. "I did quite well out of
that job at Redgarth. But talking of your Mrs. Gambrell, it's
your impression, is it, that she knows this lad, Simon Prescott?"

So he had been turning it over in his mind from the time
that I had told him of my encounter with her.

"I did rather think so," I said. "As soon as I told her that
Sue Lockett had a boy-friend who got into fights and just
might be the young man who delivered the thousand pounds
to Mrs. Bulpitt, her whole manner changed and she couldn't
wait for me to go upstairs to see Julia."

"You said you mentioned his name."

"Yes, I did."

"And was that when her manner changed?"

"I think perhaps it was."

"So we can assume she knows him, though perhaps she

didn't know of his connection with the Lockett girl, and for
some reason he's important to her. Could he have been a
former boy-friend of hers? If her life was really of the kind
she implied, there may have been quite a number of men in
it."

"It's possible, though he seems a bit young for her."

"That needn't mean anything. I've some friends who've
been very happily married for at least thirty years and she's at
least twenty years older than he is."

Felix's friends are a curious collection. He seems ready to
like anyone who shows any signs of liking him, so from
pickpockets to canons of the Church of England, from successful and hardworking actors to unemployed drunks who
have regularly to be scraped off the pavement, there is no
guessing what the background may be of someone to whom
he has chosen to introduce one. Such a very minor eccentricity as that of a man choosing to marry and live happily with
a woman twenty years his senior caused me no surprise.

"Only for some reason it doesn't seem to fit," I said. "I'm
not sure why. I suppose she just could be jealous of Sue, if
there's an affair going on between her and the boy."

"Or she might be scared at hearing he's in Allingford,"
Felix said.

"Because he could tell her husband something about her.
Only I think her husband already knows all there is to
know."

The doorbell rang.

"I'll go," Felix said. "It's probably the police again."

But it was not the police. The person whom he brought
into the room was Sue Lockett.

She was in her jeans and T-shirt and a leather jacket, so like
what Simon had worn that it might have been thought that

she had borrowed his clothes. Her hair, as it had been when I had seen her before, was tied back from her face in a ponytail. Her square, determined chin was jutting forward, her big dark eyes were ablaze with anger.

"It's all lies!" she said. "Every word of it's lies!"

"Take it easy," Felix said, "and sit down. The fact is we don't know what you're talking about. Who's been telling lies?"

"Everyone," she said. She looked unsure as to whether or not she wanted to accept his invitation to sit down. For a moment she stood with her legs straddled and her hands thrust deep into the pockets of her jacket, then she plumped down abruptly into the nearest chair. She glowered at me. "You know what I'm talking about, don't you?"

"Frankly, no," I said.

"Those jewels. She said I took them, didn't she? It's all lies."

"Mrs. Creed's jewels?" I asked. "You didn't take them?"

"If you can call them jewels. No, I didn't."

"Then who did?"

"How should I know?"

"What about Simon? He was in the house."

"But not in her room. He never went upstairs. No, it's the old woman herself had them and then said I'd taken them."

"Why should she do that?" Felix asked.

"Ever heard of insurance?"

"You think she pretended they'd been stolen so that she could claim the insurance on them?" Felix said.

"Isn't that obvious?"

"Not to me, actually. It seems out of character. And you've seen them, haven't you? You seem to have found out they aren't very valuable."

"Well, it's true, I have," she admitted without seeming to be much worried about it. "In my kind of job you've got to know things like that. I mean, the first thing I do when I take on a new job is have a very good look round. You never know what you're going to be asked to do, so at least it's best to get to know where everything is. Some people might call it being nosey, but really it's just so that you can know where you can lay your hands on things, if that's what you get asked to do."

"You thought Mrs. Creed might want you to dress her up in her jewellery, did you?" Felix said.

"No, of course not," she said impatiently. "I was just looking through the drawers in her dressing-table in case she was going to want a handkerchief or some hair-curlers or something. Sometimes the ladies I look after want me to do their hair for them. And there in one of her drawers was a jewel-case. Yes, all right, looking into it was just curiosity, and I saw there were one or two rings that might have been valuable, but the rest of it was junk, the kind of thing you pick up on holidays and so on. Anyway, I never touched a thing and wouldn't have even if it had been worth ever so much."

"If it really had no value," Felix said, "it wouldn't have been insured for much, would it?"

She gave him a blank look, as if this were something that had not occurred to her.

"Perhaps it wasn't her then," she said. "Someone might have broken into the house while she was in hospital and swiped the lot while there was no one there."

"Mr. Creed was there most of the time," he said.

"Not *all* the time, I was told they had a dog and he'd have had to be taken out for walks, wouldn't he? And he'd have visited her in hospital too. There'd have been lots of time when the house was empty."

"That's true," Felix said, "though perhaps there'd have been some signs of a break-in. But if you weren't making off with the jewellery, just why did you leave?"

"Because I don't like being insulted."

"Mrs. Creed insulted you?" I said. "I can't believe it."

"She did then!" she flashed back. "She told me I looked sloppy and mucky and she didn't think I was fit to look after the house. She said my finger-nails were dirty. She said I hadn't any self-respect."

I could just imagine that Julia might have said this, though I thought it was probably an exaggeration of what had actually passed between the two of them.

"Didn't she just say you'd look nicer in a pretty dress, or something like that?" I said. "I know she's old-fashioned."

"And where did she think I was going to get the money to pay for a pretty dress?" she demanded. "D'you know what things like that cost nowadays? I've got one or two of them at home, I admit, but I don't wear them when I'm doing a job of cooking and house-cleaning. The fact is, she didn't like me and she wanted to get rid of me and so I went. But I didn't take her bloody jewellery."

Her story just could have been true. I was half-inclined to believe it. I knew that Julia had not liked her and might have said something critical which the girl had taken more seriously than Julia had intended. But there were one or two holes in her story. Felix had noticed them too.

"If a burglar came into the house while Mr. Creed was out," he said, "why didn't he just take the rings and leave what you call the junk behind? And why didn't he help himself to anything else in the house? He didn't, did he?"

"Not that she ever said," the girl answered.

"But aren't there any oddments of any value at all there? Some silver, for instance. You can get money for its sterling value, even if it isn't antique, or anything of that sort."

"How would I know a thing like that?" she asked. "She never said anything was missing."

"And she didn't discover her jewellery was missing until after you'd left the house, did she, so she wouldn't have discovered much else, I suppose. But tell us something else now. Just why did you come here tonight to tell my wife and me about your innocence? What do you think we've got to do with the affair?"

"Mrs. Freer's one of her best friends, isn't she?" the girl said. "I thought Mrs. Creed would have told her the story and I could tell her my side of things without having to go back and talk to Mrs. Creed. I didn't want to do that. Besides it was you told the police about Mrs. Creed saying I'd taken her jewellery, wasn't it? It was you put the police on to me. That's why they came, asking me where I'd been between twelve and two o'clock yesterday. They wanted my alibi for Mrs. Bulpitt's murder. I ask you! 'Where were you,' they said, 'between twelve and two o'clock, and where was your boy-friend?' I told them what I thought of them, let me tell you! Like I said, I won't be insulted."

"And where were you?" Felix asked.

For a moment I thought that she was going to fly at him. Her fingers curled, as if she were preparing to claw at his face. But then suddenly she burst into a guffaw of laughter.

"If you could see yourself!" she said. "Trying to pretend you're some bloody detective, just like that man Dawnay. 'Where were you?' he said. Well, I was with my friend at the Rose and Crown. We had a drink or two and then we had lunch, and if it matters so much to you, you can go there and ask Walter, who works in the bar. He'll remember us."

"Not because Simon got into another fight there," Felix said. "He didn't get a second black eye."

"Not in the Rose and Crown!" she answered as if the thought of this amused her immensely. "Simon knows how to behave himself in a place like that."

"It's different in the Red Lion, is it?"

"Well, naturally. But sending for the police, like they did, was just stupid. If they'd emptied a bucket of cold water over his head it would have calmed him down."

"You seem to have an excellent understanding of him," Felix said.

"That's right, I have. He's all right if you handle him right. Well, I'll be going. But if the police come asking you any more questions about that jewellery, you can tell them what I've been saying. I never touched the stuff and I don't believe myself it was ever really stolen."

She stood up and went with swinging strides to the door.

Felix saw her out. As he came back into the room I stood up too and, looking at myself in the mirror above the fireplace, thought that if we were going to have dinner at the Rose and Crown I must really do something about some make-up. Not that it was the grandest of hotels, but it had a quiet air of luxury which always made me feel, when I went there, that I ought to be wearing something a little special. We now had two reasons for going there, of course. Felix would no doubt want to check that Sue and Simon had really had their lunch there, as well as trying to find out something about, or even to encounter, Mrs. Bulpitt's photographer nephew.

"How much of that did you believe?" he asked me as he came in.

"Hardly any of it," I said. "The girl's a complete liar."

"You think she took the jewellery?" he said.

"Don't you?"

"I suppose so. Yes, she must have. Though why she bothered to come here to tell us she hadn't is still a bit of a mystery, in spite of her explanation. If the police have already been on to her about it, but she's managed to put them off and get rid of the stuff already, I'd have thought her best course would have been to stay as quiet about it as possible."

"Well, I'm going to change," I said. "If we're going out to dinner I'd like to be presentable."

I went upstairs. I had an almost new dress with the new hem-line which I thought that I should like to wear, and of course I could put on Felix's ear-rings. But first I wanted a shower. I undressed, went to the bathroom, and was under the shower, beginning to feel pleasantly refreshed and relaxed, when I heard the telephone in my bedroom start to ring.

It was an extension of the one in the sitting-room and I thought that Felix would probably answer it downstairs, but as it went on ringing I realised that he was making no attempt to do so. Annoyed with him for leaving it to me, I got out from under the shower, clutched a bath-towel round me, and went to my bedroom.

"Virginia?" Julia Creed's voice said when I picked up the telephone. "Virginia, please tell me, and please be absolutely truthful, did you notice anything peculiar about me when you called in this afternoon?"

"Peculiar, Julia? No, of course not," I said. "Actually I thought you were looking a bit better than yesterday."

132 E. X. FERRARS

"Yes, but was there anything odd about me? I mean, anything strange?"

Her voice shook a little as she spoke.

"What's the trouble, Julia?" I asked. "What's upset you?"

"It's just that I'm wondering . . . You see, anaesthetics have some very queer after-effects, haven't they? I've often heard people say so. And then they fill you up with drugs and you don't know quite what they're doing to you. I know I had some very strange experiences while I was in the hospital. They were all ever so kind, but I know I went quite peculiar at times. For instance, one night I got out of bed and started wandering up the ward and the night nurse came and asked me what I wanted and I said I'd been invited to a party but I couldn't find where it was. Can you imagine it, me thinking I'd been invited to a party in the hospital? And she asked me where I thought I was—isn't it strange, I remembered it all perfectly in the morning?—and I said I was in Merthyr Tydvil. Don't ask me why I said Merthyr Tydvil. I've never been there, I don't know anyone there, I don't even know just where it is, except of course that it's in Wales. And she said I was in hospital in Allingford and that there weren't any parties going on there, and what I needed was to go back to bed and get some sleep. I thought she was ever so stupid because she couldn't understand me, but really she was being very kind. I think it's one of the strangest things that's ever happened to me."

"Lots of people do weird things after operations," I said. "There's no need for you to worry about it. You haven't had any other delusions that have upset you, have you?"

"That's just it," she answered. "I'm not sure I haven't. If it weren't for that crazy business in the hospital I'd never have thought of such a thing, but as it is . . . Do you think the drugs and the shock of the operation and then—then poor Malcolm—could still be making me have delusions, Virginia?"

Who was I to offer an opinion? I have a little basic medical knowledge, but not very much.

"What's the delusion you think you've had?" I asked.

"Perhaps it isn't a delusion at all. Perhaps it's something that really happened."

"Only it's so strange." She paused. I waited for her to go on, which after a moment she did. "Tell me if it's true that I came over to see you yesterday evening and told you that girl Sue Lockett had disappeared with all my jewellery."

"Yes, you did."

"I really did?"

"Yes."

"Oh dear, I was half-hoping you'd say I'd only imagined it, because you see she didn't steal anything. It's all there, every bit of it."

I was slow, trying to make up my mind how to answer. The visit of Sue Lockett and her accusation that Julia had taken and hidden her own jewellery made it seem possible that that was just what she had done. Julia's fear that it was a delusion that the jewellery had been stolen might be well founded. Not that she would have done such a thing for any reason as rational as the obtaining of the insurance on it. What her motive might have been it was impossible to guess; perhaps it had been a trick that her wandering mind had devised for getting rid of Sue. But I found it difficult to believe in that.

"You've found the jewellery in the jewel-case where you've always kept it, have you?"

"Yes," she said.

"And all arranged as it always was?"

"Well, no, that's the odd thing, it's all in a muddle. So you see I must have taken it out and hidden it somewhere and then convinced myself it had been stolen. And then sometime today, though I can't remember when, I must have dumped it back all anyhow in the case and presently come to my senses and realised what a stupid thing I'd told you about it. Or is it now that I'm being stupid, Virginia? I mean, did that girl really steal it and then for reasons of her own, like finding out, for instance, that it wasn't worth much, brought it back? Could that have happened?"

"I think it's likelier than that you imagined the whole thing," I said. "I can't explain it, but I'm sure that when you were here yesterday evening you were mentally absolutely normal, and so you were this afternoon."

"You aren't just saying that to reassure me?"

"No, honestly not."

"You don't think I ought to tell our doctor about it?"

"I'd say that depends a little on the kind of man he is."

"Oh, he's a very nice man, very level-headed."

"Then I'd tell him the whole story. It may help to take a load off your mind. But my belief is that Sue Lockett did steal the jewellery and then brought it back. Why she did that is a mystery, but I find it much easier to believe that that's what happened than that there's anything serious the matter with your mind."

"Thank you, dear. You don't know what a relief it is to know you don't think I'm going mad. You'll come and see me again soon, won't you? Good night."

She rang off.

I finished dressing, put on a little make-up and Felix's earrings, and went downstairs.

I told him about my call from Julia. He looked thoughtful, but did not say much, except that he was quite sure that I had been right that Sue Lockett had stolen the jewellery, brought it back, then come over to see us and say that Julia had been lying about her; though he had no suggestion just then as to why the girl should have done such things.

We went to the Rose and Crown in my car with me driving. The hotel is an old building in the main square of Allingford, with a very pleasant Georgian facade, but once you are inside you find that you have stepped into a much earlier age, in which ceilings had been low, supported by heavy beams, and the dark, polished floors uneven. Some of the beams, I have always believed, had been added to the structure fairly recently, to increase the sense of the picturesque, and there was concealed lighting among them which shed a somewhat dim light on the tables in the dining-room. I have always had a preference for being able to see what I am eating, but the general effect is attractive in its way.

We went into the bar before entering the dining-room. There were only a few people there. Felix ordered our drinks and we sat down at one of the low tables, waiting for them to be brought.

"Of course," Felix remarked after what had been a fairly long silence, "if the girl did take the jewellery back, there's only one way she could have done it."

"I've been trying to think about that," I said. "How did she dodge Mrs. Gambrell?"

"She didn't. They were in it together. She handed the stuff in to Mrs. Gambrell, who waited for a time until Julia came downstairs, then popped upstairs and dumped it all back in the jewel-case. Just why she did it I couldn't tell you, but to go by what you told me of your talk with her, she's somehow connected with those two, Sue Lockett and Simon Prescott, and probably she got on to the phone to Sue as soon as you went upstairs to have your talk with Julia, and told her to bring the jewellery back immediately. So the girl did what she was told and afterwards came over to tell us that Julia's accusation was all a lie. Probably that was on Mrs. Gambrell's instructions. My guess would be that Mrs. Gambrell's reason for what she did was that after the murder she didn't want the police investigating Sue and Simon too closely. Particularly Simon, to go by what you've told me. But that's only a guess."

Just then the bar-man arrived with our drinks. Felix paid him, then, looking up at him, said suddenly, "Is your name Walter?"

"That's right," the man answered, looking pleased that he was apparently becoming known in the neighbourhood.

"Were you here yesterday at lunch-time?" Felix asked.

"That's right," the man said again.

"Do you happen to know a man called Prescott, who's got a black eye at the moment, and a girl-friend called Sue?"

"Prescott, is that his name?" the man said. "I remember the young fellow with the black eye. Friends of yours?"

"They told us they'd had a good lunch here and recommended us to come," Felix lied easily.

"I don't know about them having lunch, but they had a few drinks, that I remember. More than enough for people who were going to drive." The man gave Felix a shrewd and thoughtful look. "Detectives, are you?"

Felix looked put out. He had thought that his curiosity was not too obvious. But as the man seemed cooperative he took the simplest course, though without committing himself too deeply.

"It's true we're checking certain statements the two have made to us," he said. "Can you remember what time they came in?"

"Funny thing, I've already been asked that by Superintendent Dawnay," the man said. "As I told him, I reckon it was soon after twelve o'clock. And they hung around until maybe one. Not that I can be exact about it, you understand, but I noticed them because of that black eye and the way they were dressed. Mostly people who come in here for lunch on a Sunday dress, well, I wouldn't say formally, but not so sloppily as those two. We don't encourage that sort of thing. We like to keep the tone up. Not that there's much you can do about it if they're ready to pay for their drinks and their food. Anything more I can tell you?"

"I don't think so," Felix said. "Thank you very much."

"A pleasure," the man answered automatically, and left us.

"Now you'll have to ask them in the restaurant if the two really did have lunch there," I said. "I think I'd come into the open and say we're investigating the alibis of two suspects in a murder inquiry."

"Don't you know you can get into trouble for impersonating a policeman?"

He knows far more than I do about all the things that can get a person into trouble. But as he spoke I caught at his sleeve.

"Look!" I said. "There! Just come in at the door."

"Who?"

A man had come in and gone to the bar to order a drink.

"The man I saw coming out of Mrs. Bulpitt's gate yesterday," I said. "Her nephew, the photographer."

SEVEN

THE MAN stayed at the bar with his drink. As he had been when I had seen him last, he was wearing a loose raincoat. He was tall and very thin. He had a thin face with jutting bony features and a thin-lipped mouth. He had ordered whisky and soda and drank it with a gulping thirst, then ordered another.

I waited, feeling sure that Felix would do something about him, but he took his time to make up his mind what it should be. After a while he got up and approached the man at the bar.

"Mr. Hamlyn?" he said.

The man turned his head and gave Felix a long look.

"Police?" he asked.

It was the second time that evening Felix had been taken for a policeman. I did not know if this would strike him as a compliment or its reverse. His manner was grave.

"No," he said. "It just happens that my wife was Mrs. Bulpitt's neighbour and happened to be the person who found her body. And she was passing the house as you were coming out of it. She's just recognized you, partly, I think, because she was familiar with a photograph of you that Mrs. Bulpitt had in her sitting-room. Would you care to join us?"

"It's just curiosity on your part, is it?" the man said. He had an abrupt, rather hoarse way of speaking.

Felix smiled, as if he were almost glad to have been caught out.

"You could put it that way," he said. "The police have been in and out to talk to my wife ever since she phoned them about the murder, and we're naturally curious about what's been going on since then."

"Naturally, as you say. All right, thanks." Godfrey Hamlyn walked over to our table. "Mrs.—what did you say your name was?"

"I didn't," Felix said. "I'm sorry. It's Freer."

"Mrs. Freer," the man mumbled. "Pleased to meet you." He sat down at the table, then looked back at Felix. "You said your wife was my aunt's neighbour. Doesn't that include you?"

"Unfortunately, no," Felix answered. "We've been separated for some time. It just happened that I'm here on one of my occasional visits when I come to make sure all's going well with her."

"Give me divorce every time," Godfrey Hamlyn said. "Much better than letting things trail on. You never know what may happen if you do that. Get yourself into real trouble sometime, maybe. Not that I presume to give advice."

"You mean one might get tempted to commit bigamy?" Felix said.

The man gave a laugh, as hoarse and abrupt as his way of speaking.

"I see I'll have to be careful what I say to you. All right, go on and ask me what you want to. I don't mind. I've been over it all with the police and with one or two journalists.

You're only one in the queue. First question, was my aunt alive when I left her? Isn't that what you want to know?"

"Well, was she?" Felix asked.

"Alive and telling me she'd no money to help me out of some difficulties I'd got into. A lie. She was loaded. And she knew I knew it, isn't that kind of funny? But I wouldn't have been surprised if I'd got a cheque in the post next day. That's what she was like. She wasn't mean, but she enjoyed kicking you in the teeth if you gave her the opportunity."

"She didn't say anything to you about a thousand pounds in cash that she happened to have received that morning?" Felix asked.

"A thousand pounds? And in cash and that morning? Really? She actually had it in the house, had she? The old bitch. No, she never said a word about it."

"You did quite a bit of work for her, I believe," Felix said.

The man swallowed some of his whisky, then turned a sardonic grin on Felix.

"Now who's been telling you about that? The police? Must have been, or have you been snooping round the house yourself?"

"No, it was the police," Felix said. "That's to say, they showed us photographs of a Mrs. Gambrell and a Miss Lockett. Very nice photographs."

"Oh, sure, sure. Very artistic. But didn't they show you any of my really artistic efforts?"

"I think we've heard about them, but not actually seen them."

Godfrey Hamlyn gave another of his explosive little laughs.

"That's like her, you know, keeping them in case they'd come in useful sometime. Or maybe just because she liked them. You know, sometimes when I was there and she knew we wouldn't be interrupted, she'd dress herself up in some of her old gear and put a thick layer of make-up on her face and we'd have a smashing meal and a good many drinks and sit and talk till two in the morning. She was a grand old woman in her way. Saw me through my education and was disappointed I wouldn't go to a university but took to my photography instead. Not that she ever paid me properly for the work I did for her. But that's all forgotten now. She left me everything she had in her will, and that means I won't have to do another hand's turn of work unless I want to. And I know, I know—don't say it!—that gives me a motive for hitting her on the head with a hammer, and that must have happened right after I saw her. I'd motive and opportunity, none better."

"What about means?" Felix asked. "Was she really hit on the head with a hammer?"

"Didn't the police tell you that? Yes, that's how it was done."

"Was the hammer left there?"

"Yes, and it belonged there too. It had her fingerprints on it, and there was an empty space on a rack of tools that she had on the kitchen wall where the hammer just fitted."

"So the murder wasn't premeditated. The murderer simply snatched up a weapon he'd found."

"That's how it looks."

Felix nodded thoughtfully. "But if she'd a visitor, I wonder what they were doing in the kitchen, because that's where the body was found."

I joined the discussion. "Perhaps it was something to do with the thousand pounds. When she took it out of the room we were in to put it somewhere safe, that might have been somewhere in the kitchen. She could have put it into some cupboard or canister or biscuit-box. And when she went to get the money, her visitor could have followed her out and murdered her as soon as he saw where she'd put it."

"That would have meant he knew she'd got it," Felix said. "Who besides you would have known it?"

"The person who brought it," I said.

He looked mildly startled, as if it had not occurred to him before that I could contribute something so constructive to the discussion. But then he shook his head.

"He might not have known what was in the package he was delivering."

"Then the person who sent it," I said.

This time he nodded. "Yes, it might have been either. And he killed her to get it back. But if he meant to do that, why did he bother to send it? Why shouldn't he simply have carried out his murder without producing any money? I somehow have a feeling we're wandering off the point."

The swing-doors of the bar opened and closed and Dr. Gambrell came in.

As he went to the bar I did not try to draw his attention to me, but he recognized me and came over to our table.

"Mrs. Freer?" he said. "We met yesterday, and my wife's told me she's met you since then."

"At Mrs. Creed's," I said. "It's very good of her to have taken on the job." I introduced Felix and Godfrey Hamlyn. The doctor gave each of them an austere little nod which seemed only just to acknowledge their existence, yet his shrewd, slightly bulging eyes gave them both the kind of look that suggested he would know them again if ever they should happen to meet.

"So sorry about your wife," Godfrey Hamlyn said. "Fearful tragedy."

"I beg your pardon," Dr. Gambrell said, looking puzzled.

"Your wife. No, for God's sake, what am I talking about?" Hamlyn said. "Slip of the tongue. It was Mrs. Freer mentioning your wife got me mixed up. I was thinking of poor old Creed and I'm right, I believe, that your wife's helping the widow. She's a friend of yours, isn't she?"

"I never met the lady," the doctor replied. "A tragedy, of course. Perhaps an even greater tragedy than the murder we're all talking about so much, though not quite so melodramatic."

"I don't suppose there's any money connected with the old man's death," Hamlyn said. "Is there?"

"I really don't know," the doctor said.

"There's a good deal of money coming to me from my aunt," Hamlyn remarked.

"I congratulate you," Dr. Gambrell said coldly.

"You didn't know her, I suppose," the photographer went on.

"I met her once or twice on committees to which we both belonged, that was as far as my knowledge of her went."

"Ah. Pity. You'd have liked her."

What grounds he had for saying such a thing I did not know, and Dr. Gambrell did not look interested. With a brief nod to us all, he went back to the bar, swallowed the drink that had been waiting for him there, and left.

"Well, I'd better be going too," Hamlyn said. "Nice meeting you. Hope we'll meet again sometime."

He stood up and wandered out after the doctor.

Felix and I finished our drinks, then went into the diningroom.

In its dim light we studied the menu, ordered, and then sat silent. I was waiting for him to let me know what he had in mind, but when he spoke he took me by surprise.

"I think I'll go home tomorrow," he said.

"Why should you do that?" I asked.

"You're tired of having me around," he said. "I know the signs."

"But really I'm not," I said. "Stay as long as you like."

He shook his head. "You're getting bored with me. I'll go tomorrow."

"Without solving our mystery?"

He smiled at me sadly. He could look touchingly sad when he chose.

"I didn't come to solve any mystery," he said. "I came to see how you were. I know I needn't have troubled about that. You're always all right. Even with death in the street and murder next door, you're all right as usual. And the police will solve the mystery without any assistance from me."

"You're probably right about that," I said, "but it isn't like you to give in without a struggle. What is it you really want, Felix? Is it just that I should press you to stay? I'll do that, if you like. Do stay. Honestly, it's been a help having you here while all these horrors have been happening."

"Do you really mean that?"

"Do I often say things I don't mean?"

"No, that's just the hell of it. If you were a little more insincere you'd be much easier to get on with. Tell me something. I've often wondered about it. Why haven't you wanted to marry again?"

"Perhaps I have."

"There've been other men, haven't there?"

"One or two."

"Then why haven't you thought of marrying? You know we can fix up a divorce any time you want."

I did not want to tell him the real reason why I had never wanted to marry again. It was because, though I had been somewhat in love once or twice since he and I had parted, I had never felt anything approaching what I had felt for him in the first year or so of our marriage. And if that could not be reproduced, or surpassed, why should I have troubled to turn some mildly agreeable relationship into anything as fundamental as a marriage?

"Talking of divorce," I said, "and bigamy, do you think our friend Mr. Hamlyn really made a slip of the tongue when he spoke of Mrs. Bulpitt as Dr. Gambrell's wife?"

"No," Felix said. "Did you?"

"I didn't know what to make of it."

We were interrupted at that point by the arrival of the soup that we had ordered. A pretty young girl brought it. She was just turning away when Felix called her back.

"Please forgive the question," he said, "but were you working here yesterday at lunch-time?"

I could see, from the sudden blankness of her face, which had had an attractive smile on it, that like the bar-man she had immediately placed us as detectives.

"What if I was?" she asked.

"Just checking on something," Felix said, playing the part that she expected of him. "No need to get worried about it. We want to be sure whether a young couple, names of Prescott and Lockett, had lunch here yesterday."

"I couldn't tell you, I'm sure," she said.

"But you were here yourself, were you?"

"Yes."

"But the names don't mean anything to you?"

"Do I know your names?" she asked. "I don't have to ask our guests their names, I only know our regulars."

"Well, they were both in their fairly early twenties," Felix said, "and both were dressed in jeans and leather jackets. And she had dark brown hair, tied back in a pony-tail, and he . . ." He stopped and looked at me questioningly. I remembered that he had never seen Simon Prescott.

"Fair hair, standing up in a sort of tuft on his forehead," I said.

The girl shrugged her shoulders.

"Maybe, I couldn't say. I didn't wait on them."

"Don't you think you might have noticed them if they'd come in, even if you weren't waiting on them?"

"That's what that other detective, the small, dark one with the queer eyes, wanted to know," she said. "He questioned us all, but nobody could tell him anything. Sunday lunch-time was pretty busy. There were several young people in here, but whether they had leather jackets or pony-tails or tufts on their foreheads I couldn't possibly say." Her tone had become ironic. "Is there anything else you want to know? Your soup's getting cold."

"True," Felix said, picking up his spoon. "Well, thank you."

After that it did not surprise me much that our service for the rest of the meal deteriorated.

We had reached the fruit salad at the end of it before we returned to Godfrey Hamlyn's slip of the tongue. It was after a longish silence that Felix suddenly said, "After all, it isn't impossible, is it, that Gambrell was married to Mrs. Bulpitt."

"I suppose more improbable things have happened," I said.

"It might help to explain why she came to live in Allingford when she got out of prison," he said. "She could keep him under her eye and perhaps draw a nice steady pension from him."

"She told us she was born here and lived here till she was twenty and that that was why she came back," I said.

"At which time he'd only have been about thirteen or fourteen, I should think, so they didn't get married before she left. But perhaps he knew her and got attached to her and they got married soon after he went to London, if that was where he went, as a medical student. I wonder how much Mrs. Gambrell knows about it all."

"You know, even if he was once married to Mrs. Bulpitt, it doesn't necessarily mean that his marriage to Mrs. Gambrell's bigamous," I said. "There might have been a divorce."

He nodded. "That's true. And if so, Mrs. Bulpitt wouldn't have had any hold on him, would she?"

"What makes you think she may have had a hold on him?"

"Mostly his reaction when I blackmailed him."

"Oh," I said. "We've got back to that, have we?"

He gave a sigh as he scraped a last slice of banana from his plate.

"I know your definition of blackmail is extorting money with menaces," he said, "and I didn't do that; all the same, I feel that what I did had almost the same effect as if I had. He *thought* I was going to demand money with menaces. Isn't that almost the same as if I'd actually done it?"

"So you think it was he who sent that thousand pounds to Mrs. Bulpitt?"

"I'm sure of it."

"You mean he assumed it was Hamlyn speaking?"

"That's how it looks to me. They weren't exactly friendly when they met in the bar, were they? And then Hamlyn

made his so-called slip of the tongue, with a very unconvinc-
ing explanation to account for it."

"I suppose you're right," I said hesitantly. "But there's an
awful lot of supposition about it."

"The question is, do we tell the police about that slip of
the tongue?"

"I imagine it would be very difficult to repeat exactly
what was said. I'm not sure that I could do it. Could you?"

"Perhaps not."

I felt a considerable reluctance to talk to the police about
anything, particularly something that in its way was so nebu-
lous. In the end we did not decide what we were going to do.
Felix paid the bill and we drove home and did not discuss the
matter on the drive. When we got home I made coffee, and I
believe that if Superintendent Dawnay and Sergeant Wells
had not called on me that evening we might have managed to
forget most of what had happened earlier in the Rose and
Crown.

The two detectives came in, looking if anything more
sombre than usual, but they seemed glad to accept some coffee when I offered it to them. They were very tired-looking
men. I had stirred up what was left of the fire, and the
superintendent remarked that it was nice to see a real fire, it
gave life to a room. The sergeant, who as far as I could
remember had said almost nothing since I had first met him,
suddenly exclaimed that they made a lot of work and dirt and
did not really warm a room anything to compare with central heating. The superintendent replied that he knew the new
police houses had central heating, but give him a real old-
fashioned fire any time, as he had in his own home.

I thought the two men were going to have a really heated
argument about which was best. Each looked irritably deter-

mined to defend his own point of view. But then the sergeant, attempting conciliation, said that what you really needed was both, as I obviously had, because of course if there was a blizzard and the power-lines came down the central heating went off with the electricity, and then where were you if you hadn't got a fire? The superintendent looked satisfied, as if he had won a victory. I thought that what they both needed was a rest and that meanwhile my coffee might help.

Suddenly Dawnay turned his pale eyes on me and asked, "Did you get any useful information this evening, Mrs. Freer?"

So they knew that we had been to the Rose and Crown and asking questions.

"Have you been following us?" I asked, a little astonished because it gave me an unfamiliar feeling of importance. I could not remember ever having been followed by the police before.

"We weren't following you," Dawnay said. "We had a man in the Rose and Crown, keeping an eye on Hamlyn, and he reported that you had what appeared to be a very interesting conversation with him. Our man also reported that you were joined for a few minutes by Dr. Gambrell, also that you questioned one of the waitresses in the restaurant about the alibis of Prescott and Lockett. Of course I can't stop you if you choose to do that sort of thing. It can't be called obstructing the police. But I would like to discourage it."

"I'm sorry if we've been getting in the way," Felix said. "However, I think we may have chanced on something that may interest you. When the doctor was talking to us, Hamlyn produced what he claimed was a slip of the tongue. We

thought it deliberate. He referred to Mrs. Bulpitt as Dr. Gambrell's wife."

"Ah yes," Dawnay said. "Perfectly correct."

"So you know about that, do you?" Felix said, disappointed. "His present marriage is bigamous."

"We aren't absolutely certain of it yet," Dawnay answered,
"but it seems probable. Among Mrs. Bulpitt's papers, which
she kept in a most methodical way, is a marriage certificate,
dated about twenty years ago, between an Adela Bulpitt and
a Denis Gambrell, and there's no paper relating to a divorce.
But of course that doesn't mean for sure that there was no
divorce. A paper can get mislaid, even by someone as busi-
nesslike as Mrs. Bulpitt. We shall have to check divorce
records. But that isn't what we came to see you about, Mrs.
Freer. It's about something that may be trivial, but it's odd.
Can you tell me anything about the mental state of your
friend Mrs. Creed?"

"Oh," I said. "You want to know about the jewellery."

"So you do know something about it?"

"I'm not sure that I really *know* anything," I said, "but I
believe that Mrs. Creed is perfectly sane. She's worried herself
about her state of mind, but I don't think she has any reason
to be."

"Did she hide her own jewellery and accuse the Lockett
girl of having stolen it?"

"Is that what she told you herself?"

"Yes, a little while ago. She telephoned us and told us she
thought it was her duty to tell us that she now thought that
Susan Lockett was perfectly innocent."

"Well, I don't believe that myself," I said.

"Why not?"

"Because what I think is that Sue Lockett stole the jewellery and left the house, and Mrs. Creed discovered that it and the girl were gone and came to the very natural conclusion that the girl had stolen it. She came over here and told us about it and she seemed to us perfectly normal. Still ill, of course, shaken by the after-effects of the operation she'd had and the fearful shock of her husband's death. Then the next thing that happened was that Sue Lockett turned up here and told us the accusation was a lie."

"When did that happen?" Dawnay asked quickly.

I looked at Felix. "Did you notice what the time was?"

"Not exactly," he said. "It was before we left for the Rose and Crown, perhaps about six o'clock."

"But you saw her this evening?"

"Oh yes."

The superintendent and sergeant exchanged glances that I did not understand.

"You were both here when she came?" Dawnay asked.

"Yes," I said.

"But you didn't believe the girl."

"No."

"Why not?"

"I'm not sure why not. I just didn't. I didn't think Mrs. Creed would make an accusation of that kind without good reason. Then she telephoned me and asked me what I thought about her state of mind when I'd seen her last. It seems she'd had a rather odd experience when she was in hospital, believing she'd been invited to some party. Which of course was a complete delusion and the after-effect of the operation and the drugs she'd been given, and it had left her with a feeling of uncertainty about her own sanity, because the jewellery had all turned up again in her jewel-case. And so she was

afraid that she'd imagined everything about its being missing
and that her mind still wasn't to be trusted."

Dawnay nodded. "That's more or less what she told me.
But if you don't believe it, what do you think really happened?"

"I think Mrs. Gambrell comes into the story. You know
she's been looking after Mrs. Creed today, do you?"

"Yes."

"Well, in the afternoon, when I got home from work, I
went over to see Mrs. Creed, and Mrs. Gambrell and I had a
talk before I went upstairs to see Mrs. Creed. And . . . I
don't know quite how to put it."

He waited for me to go on. I was beginning to find his
steady gaze disconcerting.

"You see, it's only a feeling I had, it's nothing definite," I
said.

"Never mind, go on."

"It was when I started to speak about Sue's boy-friend,
Simon Prescott, that something funny seemed to happen. Her
whole manner seemed to change. She became sort of stiff and
aloof and she could hardly wait for me to go upstairs to see
Mrs. Creed. And what I think happened is that as soon as I'd
gone she rang up either Sue or Simon and told them they'd
got to bring the jewellery back. So Sue brought it back and
gave it to Mrs. Gambrell, who waited for a moment when
Mrs. Creed was out of her room, and dumped the whole lot
back in the jewel-case, not arranged in the way she'd had it
herself."

"And what do you think that means?"

"I don't know, except that it seems Mrs. Gambrell has
some connection with either Sue or Simon."

"But what was her motive? Why did Mrs. Gambrell tell

one or the other of them that they'd got to bring the jewellery back?"

"Perhaps Mrs. Gambrell just doesn't like theft."

I suddenly became extremely aware of the ear-rings that I was wearing. It was perfectly possible that Felix had paid for them and they were legally mine, but it just could be that I was the receiver of stolen property. He did not look in any way concerned himself.

"If Mrs. Gambrell doesn't like theft," Dawnay said, "perhaps she doesn't like murder either."

I did not feel this required a reply, but Felix had something to say.

"There's another possible reason why Mrs. Gambrell might have wanted to have that jewellery returned," he observed. "She may not have wanted the police to take too much interest in Sue Lockett at the moment, as they'd probably be doing after Mrs. Creed's accusation, and Mrs. Gambrell's reason for that could be the girl's connection with Prescott. He obviously means something to her. And what might really be worrying her now might have something to do with Mrs. Bulpitt's murder."

"Would you care to explain that?" Dawnay said cautiously.

"No, I can't really," Felix said. "It's just a thought."

"I sometimes have thoughts like that," Dawnay said, "and they turn out to be wrong about ninety-nine percent of the time."

"There's always that remaining one percent," Felix said. "Meanwhile there's something I rather want to tell you about. It just might change the odds a little."

The two men looked as if they were just preparing to go. I wondered what Felix was going to come up with now. What

I was not prepared for was the fact that he had just made up his mind to tell them the truth.

"I've done something that I feel I ought to tell you about," he said. "It was on Saturday I took Creed's dog for a walk— my wife had been looking after him for Mrs. Creed—and we got to a place called Durkin Square. And there, among all the other cars parked round the square, was a silver-grey Jaguar, and the last letters on its number-plate were VTF. And the fact is, just as I arrived here on Friday evening, I saw a silver-grey Jaguar taking off from in front of this house, or it might have been the house next door, and the only thing I noticed about it as it drove off were the letters on the number-plate, VTF. I remember it because I said to myself, 'That stands for "Very Thick Fog,"' which somehow made sense, because if you remember, the evening was very foggy."

"Just a minute," Dawnay said. "Are you telling me you actually saw the accident in which Mr. Creed was killed?"

"I must have, mustn't I?" Felix said. "But I didn't take it in. All I saw was this car coming swerving out from the side of the street, and after it had gone there was something lying in the road and a lot of people, who I suppose had heard the noise of it, come rushing out to look at it. And I saw my wife amongst them, and I knew she'd be surprised to see me here, so I stood and waited till she noticed me. But it's Saturday morning I want to tell you about, not Friday. It was on Saturday that I saw this car in Durkin Square with the letters VTF on the number-plate, and I thought, 'I believe that could be the car I saw on Friday,' and I went to look at the brass plate beside the door of the house in front of which it was parked. Nearly all the houses there have brass plates by their doors. The square seems to be a nest of doctors. And this one said Dr. Denis Gambrell. Of course, I couldn't be sure that

was where the car belonged, with parking congestion being
what it is, so I thought I'd check. There may be lots of silver-
grey Jaguars with the letters VTF on their number-plates. So
I went to a telephone box, got Directory Inquiries to give me
Dr. Gambrell's number, and rang him up."

He paused for so long that Dawnay, who had become
noticeably more alert than he had been when he came into
the house, said, "And then?"

"I'll tell you what I think happened then," Felix said, "but
my memory isn't all that reliable. When he answered I simply
said, 'Ellsworthy Street.' That was all at first. And then he
said absolutely nothing. He didn't ask me who I was or what
I was talking about or anything like that. There was just
silence. So then I said something like, 'People like you should
pay for what they've done.' And he simply rang off. But next
morning, you see, Mrs. Bulpitt received a mysterious anonymous gift of a thousand pounds."

"Which has mysteriously vanished," Dawnay said. His
voice was dry. He did not seem much impressed. "If it was
ever there."

"My wife saw it," Felix said in a tone of offence.

"Now wait a minute, please," Dawnay said. "Your belief is
that Dr. Gambrell took your telephone call as the beginning
of blackmail, because you, or whoever he thought was calling
him, had seen him drive away from in front of Mrs. Bulpitt's
house, run over Malcolm Creed, and drive on without stopping."

Felix nodded. "But you understand, all I was actually doing was checking that I'd identified the right car."

"As you thought you had."

"It does seem probable, doesn't it?"

"Then why didn't you tell us about this a bit sooner?"

"Because I'd no proof. Even now that I'm telling you about it you don't really believe Gambrell sent Mrs. Bulpitt that thousand pounds, do you, though to me it's as clear as day. I think he thought that telephone call had come from that nephew of hers, Hamlyn, and he thought that with luck he could buy her off with a thousand pounds. But I think that after my wife left the house Mrs. Bulpitt telephoned him and said a thousand wasn't nearly enough and he'd better do better. So after he'd been to the Gleesons' party he came here, just missed meeting Hamlyn who'd been in to visit his aunt, argued with her about the money, and when she wouldn't listen to him, he killed her. That seems to me to be logical."

"Logic!" Dawnay said bitterly. "As if it ever got one anywhere. When the human being begins to behave logically we're really in for trouble. I suppose you think he took his thousand pounds away with him."

"Possibly," Felix said.

"It just happens, unfortunately, that he's got an alibi for the time of Mrs. Bulpitt's murder. He was having lunch with a colleague. However, thank you for your information, Mr. Freer. It's certainly of great interest."

"Only I don't think you believe a word of it," Felix said.

Dawnay stood up. "Oh, I believe it. It's only about the conclusions you've drawn from it that I'm in doubt. There are questions you haven't answered. For instance, will Hamlyn's corpse be the next one we have to deal with? If you're right, Hamlyn must have been told by his aunt about the Jaguar being in Ellsworthy Street. Incidentally, why was it there? What was Dr. Gambrell doing visiting Mrs. Bulpitt? If I were in Hamlyn's shoes I should proceed from now on very, very carefully."

"It may be what he's doing," Felix said.

"True. Well, as I said, thank you for your help."

Every time that I had met Superintendent Dawnay he had always thanked me for my help, though I had never been sure of what the help consisted. He and the sergeant left together.

When they had gone and Felix had closed the front door behind them, he came back, dropped down on the sofa, stretched out wearily, and lit a cigarette.

"You look tired," I said. "Is telling the truth very exhausting?"

"It is when you're trying to remember what not to say."

"So you don't believe half of what you said yourself?"

"Oh, I believe all of it, but there were certain things I didn't trouble to mention."

"Such as?"

"Nothing important."

"I'd like to know what made you suddenly tell them all that rigmarole."

He did not answer at once; then he said, "It was all perfectly true about my telephone call, you know, in case you've had doubts about it, and we've agreed it wasn't extorting money with menaces."

"But the rest of it," I said. "That Dr. Gambrell sent the thousand pounds and that he murdered Mrs. Bulpitt. Why did you say all that?"

"To see how it sounded."

"And how do you think it sounds, now that you know he's got an alibi?"

"I'm not sure. Perhaps it does. But it's their affair now and I can leave tomorrow without feeling I dodged a responsibility."

"It'll be about the first time you haven't done your best to do that." I stood up and went to the television. In another minute or two it would be time for the news. Before switching on I said, "Are you really going back to London tomorrow, Felix?"

"Why not?" he said. "I've told those men everything I know and I don't want to overstay my welcome here."

"You know you can stay as long as you like."

"Do you actually *want* me to stay?" he said incredulously.

I switched on the television. The first sound that came out of it was one of those dreadful roars of laughter and clapping, which drowned the answer I was trying to make to the effect that for a change it was pleasant to have company in the empty house, though I felt that I might regret this later.

Then there were one or two items of news about the Middle East and South Africa and a military coup somewhere in South America. The world seemed to be its usual grim self.

Then there came the statement that the corpse of a young woman which had been found in a wood near the town of Allingford had been identified as that of a Miss Susan Lockett. She had been killed by a number of blows on the head with a hammer. A man was being questioned.

EIGHT

FELIX AND I looked at one another. After a moment I switched the news off.

"Why didn't they tell us about it?" he said.

"Those police?"

"Yes. Of course they knew about it."

"They must have."

"They did ask us if we'd both been here when Sue Lockett came."

"Which may mean we're the last people who'll admit to seeing her alive."

"I don't like it," he said.

I did not like it much myself. Apart from not much liking murder, I did not like the fact that Superintendent Dawnay, although he had certainly known of Sue Lockett's death, had told us nothing about it.

"I suppose the man they're questioning is Prescott," Felix said.

"We can't tell, can we?" I answered. "It could be anyone out of her past, or simply someone who gave her a lift on the road."

"A girl like her would be too experienced to risk anything of that sort. No, it'll be Prescott."

But he was wrong. We found that out next morning when Sandra arrived, together with a rather solemn Louella leading Jinks with an air of great responsibility. On reaching Ellsworthy Street the old dog naturally tried to make for his home in the Creeds' house and had to be coaxed to come into mine, but once he was in he gave a friendly wag of his tail and settled down on the hearth-rug in the sitting-room as if he knew that shortly the fire would be lit.

Sandra, with her rubber gloves on and looking as neat and attractive as she always did, started sweeping out the ashes of Saturday's fire.

"Louella come in crying yesterday," she said. "She said a boy knocked her down. Jim said, 'You shouldn't cry, you should've knocked him down.' Louella said, 'What would've happened if I'd suffocated him?' Jim said, 'He'd've died.' Louella said, 'Oh.' "

It seemed to me perhaps as adequate as anything else one might think to say on the subject of attempted murder.

"How are you getting on with Jinks?" I asked.

"Fine," Sandra said. "Louella loves him. And I believe myself he's so old he doesn't much care where he is so long as he's warm and got enough to eat. Does Mrs. Creed want him back?"

"I don't think so," I said. "I think she's very grateful to you for taking him."

"How is she?"

"Getting on fairly well, considering."

"Poor lady. They still don't know nothing for sure who drove that car that killed her husband, so Jim says, though they've had a tip it might be Dr. Gambrell. Can you believe it—a man like Dr. Gambrell? I was sent to him when I had my miscarriage last year and he was ever so nice. And now they're questioning him. I said to Jim when he told me, 'The world's gone mad,' I said. A man like Dr. Gambrell wouldn't have nothing to do with a girl like that Lockett girl."

"Wait a minute," I said. She had just been about to shoot out of the room with her bucketful of ashes from the grate. "Are you saying that the man they're questioning about Sue Lockett's death is Dr. Gambrell?"

"That's right," she said.

"Not a young man called Prescott?"

"Oh, him," she said. "No, so Jim said. He was in the Red Lion as usual, got an alibi, but was quiet for once. Maybe that was because his mother was with him. But they've signs, you see, Sue Lockett was in Dr. Gambrell's car sometime. There were her fingerprints in it and some hairs they think are hers. Not that they can be sure of that so soon, but they're pretty sure of it, so they picked up Dr. Gambrell and had him along to the station for questioning, but I believe they let him go later. I'm not sure about that. Jim'll tell me about it today."

"But Simon Prescott has a mother, has he?" I asked, somehow surprised. It had not entered my head to wonder if he had a family, or to picture what kind of people they might be. Young men like him seemed poised in limbo.

"Didn't you know?" Sandra said. "He's Mrs. Gambrell's son. She used to be Mrs. Prescott before her marriage to Dr. Gambrell."

Now I was really surprised.

"Does he live with them?" I asked.

"Yes, I think so."

"What does he do?"

"Nothing much, I think. I believe he was at some university, then he come home, supposed to be looking for a job, but found life comfortable enough without one. Not that I really know. As I told you, he was always in trouble, getting into fights, and it's my opinion, if Dr. Gambrell hadn't been good friends with Major Allwood, he's chief constable, young Prescott would've got sent up before now. Not that I'd like you to repeat that. It could be I'm wrong. Jim always said Prescott would go too far one day and they'd have to charge him."

"But he wasn't the person they were questioning about Sue Lockett's death?"

"No, definitely."

Felix, who had said nothing that morning about going home that day, had been listening to our conversation. Now he remarked, "I suppose he might have had a motive for murdering the girl, but he may not have been the only one."

"I'm not going to murder anyone when I grow up," Louella announced. "It's right silly."

"You just stick to that," Felix said.

"There!" Sandra exclaimed. "I ought never to have been talking like this in front of her. She picks up everything."

"If I do murder anyone," Louella said, "what will they do to me?"

"Put you in prison for the rest of your life," her mother said.

"Will I like that?"

"You bet your life you won't. Now let's talk about something else. I've work to do."

"Could I try going to prison for a little while to see if I like it?" the child persisted.

"I'll tell you one thing, you couldn't take Jinks," Sandra said, at which Louella's face fell. It seemed that Sandra had found the way to settle the subject, for when she left the room and returned a moment later with paper and kindling to lay a new fire, Louella had lost interest in the possibilities of murder as a future career.

I went out to the hall, took my overcoat from a peg there, and put it on.

"I suppose you're going across the way to see Mrs. Creed," Felix said, following me.

"Yes, I think I'd better do that," I said. "I've been thinking . . ."

"Yes?"

"If it's true that it was Dr. Gambrell being questioned about Sue Lockett's death, is it possible that Harriet stayed with Julia? It doesn't seem likely."

"No."

"So I may have to spend most of today with her."

"Like me to do some shopping for you while you're out?"

"So after all you're staying."

"I thought that might be best, at least until we know a bit more about that girl's death. I mean, if the Jaguar's involved, I may be able to tell the police something."

"I thought you'd told them everything about identifying it yesterday," I said.

"Yes—yes, of course."

"Felix, what didn't you tell them?"

"Absolutely not a thing. Made a clean breast of everything. Now is there any shopping you'd like me to do?"

"If you're staying," I said, realising that I had never really taken seriously his intention of leaving today, "you could look around in the kitchen and see what you think we need. I imagine you'll cook some lunch."

"Yes, certainly, if you want me to."

"I know the whisky's a bit low."

"Drink!" he said disparagingly and wandered off to the kitchen.

I went out by the front door, crossing the road through the fine, cold rain that I only discovered was falling when I felt its dampness on my face. In spite of the rain there was a small crowd standing about outside Mrs. Bulpitt's gate. Sightseers, I supposed, drawn there by the heady scent of murder. I went to Julia's door and rang the doorbell.

I was taking for granted that she was alone, as I felt sure that Harriet Gambrell would have left, and that it might take Julia some time to reach the door, or even that she might not answer it at all, but it was opened almost at once by Simon. There was a peculiarly hopeless air about him, a look of desperation, as if life, in all its dreadful complexity, had suddenly become altogether too much for him. He had a tea-cloth in one hand.

"Oh, it's you," he said. "Thank the Lord!"

I thought that the warmth of this welcome must mean that he had been expecting the police and was relieved to see that it was only me, but I had misjudged him.

"She's got a dishwasher," he said, "but I don't know how to make the bloody thing work. I'm afraid if I start turning switches I'll probably smash everything there is inside it. So I'm doing all the washing-up by hand. Hell, I wasn't told about that when I said I'd come here."

"What are you doing here?" I asked.

"Looking after the old lady," he said. "My mother went home as soon as she heard—well, she went home, but she asked me to come round here this morning and do what I could. I made some breakfast, just cornflakes and coffee and so on, and I've been trying to do what I could about this bloody washing-up, but to tell you the truth, I don't think she much wants me around."

His black eye had faded to a greenish blur, but it still gave him a rather sinister appearance.

"Of course you know about Sue Lockett's death," I said.

He gave a deep sigh, seemed uncertain as to whether or not he should answer, then stood aside so that I could enter.

"That's right, I know," he said. "But I don't know about this dishwasher. Suppose you come and show me how it works."

We went to the kitchen. There was a fair amount of crockery and glass in the dishwasher, some of which it appeared he had extracted and started washing in the sink. I was not familiar with this make of dishwasher, but I thought I could guess how it worked. I put in some detergent, closed it, and turned some switches. After a slight hiccup the machine began to purr gently.

He beamed at me. "That's it. You've got it."

He threw the tea-cloth down on the table.

"So what will you be doing now?" I asked. "Going home?"

"No, I've promised I'd stay on and get some lunch and so on," he said. "What d'you think I ought to give her for lunch? I can do poached eggs quite well."

"I'll go up and ask her what she feels like," I said. "Do you know how she is?"

"Looks pretty good to me. She's old, of course. Perhaps it's harder then to get back on your feet after all this sort of trouble than it is if you're younger."

"It's good of you to come and help," I said.

"That's all right."

"You say your mother sent you."

He nodded.

"And that was after she'd heard of Sue Lockett's murder," I said.

"Yes, I told her."

"Then how did you hear of it yourself?"

He threw himself down on a chair, stretching out his legs before him.

"I don't want to talk about this," he said. "I cared for that girl. First girl I've ever cared for, as you might say, seriously. We were thinking of getting married. We only had to wait till I'd got a job of some sort. We didn't want to stay in Allingford, because we'd had enough of my family. You know old Gambrell's my stepfather, don't you? I always got on all right with my mother, but he and I always got across one another. I don't altogether blame him. He never wanted a son at all, but he'd have been all right to me, I guess, if I'd gone the way he wanted. Become another medical, or something like that. But I couldn't see much future in it. Not for me."

"What do you want to do?" I asked.

"Damned if I know. Scratch a living somehow till I find out. Maybe go to Australia, or something like that."

"You'd need a job there quite as much as you do here."

"But it'd be a long way off."

"And that's an advantage?"

"Could be."

"Did Sue want to go to Australia?"

"She didn't mind."

"You haven't told me how you heard of her murder," I said.

He gave me a long look. I had sat down by then, facing him across the table.

"The police came to the house yesterday evening," he said. "Said her body had been found in Bereford Wood. D'you know it? It's just north of Allingford. Looks as if someone drove her out along the main road, turned off it, dumped her body by the side of a track, and drove on. And for some reason they came straight to us, wanted to check the Jag, then they took it away and wanted my father—my stepfather—to go with them. Of course I came here and got hold of my mother and took her to have a drink in the Red Lion and told her about it. And we went home, then she sent me here this morning. Actually they didn't keep my father long. They think, you see, Sue's murder had something to do with the Bulpitt murder, and my father's got a complete alibi for that."

"Have you?" I asked.

His gaze on me was steady, then he gave a sudden laugh.

"You've got a nerve," he said, "sitting here with a double murderer, asking him if he's got an alibi. Suppose I was to take one of those tools over there and hit you over the head with it."

I glanced at the tool-rack on the wall, which was very like the one in Mrs. Bulpitt's kitchen. It held a screw-driver and a chisel, but there was a gap between them.

I said, "The hammer's missing."

"Is that so?" he answered calmly, as if this were a fact of which he was well aware. "Then you're safe for the moment. Stabbing someone to death with a screw-driver would be a messy business."

"Simon, please listen to me," I said. "Have you an alibi for the time of Mrs. Bulpitt's murder?"

"Well then, I believe I have," he answered. "Sue and I had lunch in the Rose and Crown. We had drinks first, then lunch, and took our time over it, so I don't think either of us had a chance of getting away to do the old lady in."

"But you'd been to her house earlier in the morning, hadn't you?" I said. "Didn't you arrive on a motorbike and deliver a package?"

He started forward in his chair. "If you think I went into the house then—"

"I don't, I don't," I said. "I was with her at the time. If it was you who delivered the package, I saw you leave without coming in. Anyway, I believe she went to church after that. I know she was meaning to go, and if she did there'll be lots of people who saw her there. But it was you who delivered the package, wasn't it?"

His grin had changed to a sullen scowl. "Yes, all right, it was."

"Who gave it to you to deliver?"

He hesitated, then gave a shrug of his shoulders. "All right, it was old Gambrell. You already know so much, I don't suppose it matters, telling you the rest. It had money in it, hadn't it? Don't ask me why he was giving it to her. I know the police think she had a hold on him, but she hadn't. They think he'd committed bigamy, marrying my mother, but actually he hadn't. He's supposed to have been married to Mrs. Bulpitt, who'd been a Miss Bulpitt when he first knew her, and she'd stuck to her old name. But the marriage wasn't legal because she'd a husband alive at the time of it. He'd run out on her and Gambrell never knew anything about him till the man died. He'd gone off to Brazil or somewhere and made a good deal of money and it somehow came to her. So then she told Gambrell about it and said she was breaking off the marriage and setting up on her own. He was only a medical student then, without any money. And that was the last he saw of her till she turned up here in Allingford. But she'd no hold on him, so why he sent her that money on Sunday I don't know."

"How long have you known all this?" I asked.

"As a matter of fact, only since yesterday afternoon."

"It was then that your stepfather told you about it for the first time, was it?"

"Yes."

"What do you think made him do that?"

"Isn't it obvious? The police had been to see him, letting him know they believed he was a bigamist. They'd found a marriage certificate among Mrs. Bulpitt's things, showing he'd been married to her, but there wasn't anything about a divorce. Naturally not, as there'd never really been a marriage. But as things looked bad for him, he thought it was time he told my mother and me the truth. He and I talked it over, but my mother was here all yesterday afternoon, but when I took her out in the evening I told her about it."

"And all of this means that your stepfather had no motive for the murder of Mrs. Bulpitt."

"Not a shadow of one."

"What about Sue Lockett? Had he any motive there? I know, I know—!" I held up my hand before he could speak. "You wouldn't tell me if he had. But do you know of anyone else who might have had one?"

His face changed from sullen hostility to bewildered dismay. It was a face, I had noticed, that could change its expression with astounding rapidity.

"Don't you think it was probably one of those maniacs one's always hearing about?" he said, his voice beginning to shake a little. "They pick girls up somehow, rape them, batter them to death, dump them by the road. That's what I think."

"Had she been raped?"

"I don't know. No, I don't think so. No, I'm sure she hadn't. The police would have said, wouldn't they?"

"I should think so. Now I'll go up to see Mrs. Creed, I think. Don't worry any more about the dishwasher. It'll turn itself off."

I left him sprawling beside the table and went upstairs to see Julia.

I expected to find her in bed still, or at least lying down, but she was fully dressed and walking about the room with nervous restlessness. She had even made her bed, at least I presumed that it was she who had done it, as it did not strike me as the kind of thing that Simon would think of doing for her. She had a glass of what looked like orange juice in her hand and she appeared stronger than she had the day before, but she had been crying.

"Come in, Virginia," she said as I paused in the doorway. "And please shut the door, because I don't want that boy listening to us."

"Why ever should he do that, Julia?" I asked, but as she wanted, closed the door.

"I don't know," she said. "That's the trouble, I don't know."

"Has he been spying on you somehow?" I asked. I could not imagine any reason why he should do such a thing.

"He did when the police came this morning— Oh, I haven't told you about that. They were here quite early and he'd just arrived and he hung about outside the door all the time they were talking to me." She gulped some orange juice. "Oh dear, if it weren't so early, I'd put some gin in this. I've been drinking pints of the stuff ever since I got home. I don't seem to be able to eat anything to speak of, but I can just manage to drink this."

"If he'd only just arrived, perhaps he was waiting for some instructions from you, not spying," I said.

"No, I'm sure he wanted to know what the police were saying to me," she said. "Do sit down, Virginia. I'm sorry there's only the one chair. They came here to ask me about a hammer we had in the kitchen. And then when they had gone I started to cry, because, you see, the hammer they've found by the girl's body has Malcolm's fingerprints on it, and that seemed to me so sad, so terribly sad. I mean, to be remembered by fingerprints on a hammer. I'm sorry, Virginia—" The tears had started again. She mopped at them with a handkerchief that already looked sodden. "I can't help it. I've hardly cried at all till now, and now I simply can't stop."

I sat down on the chair that she had indicated, the only easy-chair in the room, while she sat down abruptly on the edge of the bed, the suddenness of it making some of the orange juice slosh over the edge of the glass. It made a splash on the grey jersey dress that she was wearing, but she took no notice of it.

"You know, it isn't because of grief I'm crying," she said. "It's because I've been so lucky. Fifty-seven years we had together, think of that! We were both eighty and we knew we hadn't got long, one or other of us was going to go soon and the other be left behind, but we had fifty-seven years together. So lucky, so very lucky." She swallowed some more orange juice. "I really do wish this had some gin in it. Do you think, now that I'm alone, that I may become an alcoholic? I keep thinking of having a drink."

"If you'd really like some gin, I'll go and look for it," I said. "Have you any in the house?"

"At this time in the morning!" She looked shocked. "Oh, I couldn't possibly. But you do understand, don't you, how one can cry just because one's been so very lucky, without specially deserving it, you know, its just happening?"

I rather wanted to start crying myself, partly, no doubt, out of envy, because I had not been so lucky. My husband had not been run over by a car, but he had not been exactly a lucky number.

"You said the police came here this morning," I said. "What did they want?"

"It was about the murder of that poor girl. She was killed by blows on the head with a hammer and the hammer was there beside her when they found her and it's got Malcolm's fingerprints on it. So they came to ask me if we'd lost a hammer and of course we have. There used to be one in that rack in the kitchen, but it isn't there now. So they wanted to know when it went missing and of course I couldn't tell them. Malcolm never said anything about it when he came to visit me in the hospital, and I think he would have if it had gone then. He'd have noticed a thing like that. Virginia—" She leant forward suddenly and caught me by the sleeve. "Can you get rid of that boy? I'm frightened of him."

"Has he done anything to frighten you?" I asked. I noticed that Sue Lockett, who had been a wicked creature who stole jewellery, now that she had been murdered, had become a poor girl.

"No, no, nothing, it's just that he scares me," Julia said. "I expect it's just my nerves, but I wish he'd go."

"I'll tell him that, if you like," I said. "But then what are we going to do about you?"

"I'm all right," she said. "I can look after myself perfectly well now. If I know I can phone you if I need anything special, that's really all I want."

"Why don't you come and stay with me for a little while?" I asked.

"But you've got a visitor."

"I think he's leaving today."

"Really?" She seemed to be thinking it over.

The trouble was, I was not sure if he really was leaving or not.

"Anyway, as I told you before, that doesn't matter," I said. "You can have the room he's got at the moment and he can sleep downstairs."

"Oh, I couldn't think of letting him do that," she said. "If he does go, then perhaps . . . But we needn't decide anything now, need we? If you could just get rid of that boy . . . Or do you think I'm just being ungrateful? It was very good of him to come, I do realise that, specially when his fiancée has just been so horribly killed, though perhaps coming to do a little job like this helps him to take his mind off it. I don't want to be selfish when other people are being so good to me. If only he hadn't got that black eye!"

"It's rapidly fading," I said.

"But it keeps reminding one of how violent he must be. I mean, getting into fights in public houses, that really isn't nice, is it?"

"Not very. Tell me, Julia, did the police want to know only about when the hammer went missing?"

Her tears had stopped, at least for the moment, but the gaze of her reddened eyes was blank.

"I think it was. No, it wasn't. They wanted to know when Mrs. Gambrell left yesterday evening. I couldn't tell them. She gave me some supper, then went out to the kitchen to stack the dishwasher, she said, and I settled down for a little while to watch television, then went up to bed. I didn't hear her anywhere, so I thought she'd gone to bed too and I only realised she must have left when she didn't bring me my breakfast this morning. I waited for it for a time, then about nine o'clock I got up and got my coffee myself, and I looked in her room for her, but she wasn't there and the bed hadn't been slept in. Then that boy turned up, saying his mother wasn't well and had asked him to come instead of her. And only a few minutes after he got here Superintendent Dawnay and a sergeant arrived and started asking me questions."

"And those were the only things they wanted to know—when the hammer went missing and when Mrs. Gambrell went missing too?"

She gave me a startled look. "She isn't *missing,* is she, Virginia? Not—I mean, not missing, probably dead. That's what they used to say in the war, wasn't it? There hasn't been another accident or murder or anything terrible, has there?"

"I'm sorry, I shouldn't have put it like that," I said. "No, for all I know, she's safe at home."

"For a moment you frightened me. D'you know, that's a queer thing I've noticed about myself at the moment? I keep getting frightened of all sorts of things. I'm not really like that."

"I don't think it's so very surprising," I said. "I shouldn't worry about it. But I'll see about getting rid of Simon for you. I expect he'll be quite happy to go."

"Of course, it *was* good of him to come," she said, and I thought for a moment that she was having second thoughts about asking him to leave. But then she nodded, as if agreeing about something with herself. "Yes, it was good of him, and you could tell him I said so, and that I do appreciate it and so on—do please be very nice to him about it—but I'll be happier when he's out of the house."

I found it difficult to be very nice to Simon about dismissing him, because when I went downstairs and found him still sitting at the table in the kitchen, where I had left him, he was helplessly, hopelessly weeping.

He had his elbows on the table, his head held in his hands, and his shoulders were jerking with the violence of his sobs. I felt the acute embarrassment that a woman always feels at the sight of a man's tears. Julia's had only given me a sad feeling of helplessness at not being able to do more for her, but Simon's made me feel almost angry, as if he were assaulting me with his grief. When he saw me he extracted a rather dirty handkerchief from his pocket and mopped his face.

"I told you, I loved the bloody girl," he said, his voice husky from his crying. "Don't look at me like that. I can cry if I want to, can't I?"

"Of course," I muttered. "Only I think it would be best if you went home, I think Mrs. Creed wants to be left alone now."

"She doesn't like me, does she?"

"I think it upsets her, having a young man looking after her instead of a woman," I said, hoping this was a tactful way of putting it. "I'll look in again presently and make sure she's all right."

"Suits me. I never wanted to come."

"I'm sure she's grateful."

"I've had enough of gratitude, let me tell you. All Sue and I did was to call in to tell the old woman we were going to get married—" He stopped abruptly. His face went blotchily pale. One cheek was twitching. "That was some days ago.

She'd had some connection with the old bitch in the past and said she'd been good to her and that she'd be glad to know things were working out all right for her. And what does the old woman do out of gratitude for Sue's bothering to go and see her? Do you know what she did?"

"How can I?" I said.

"No, well, never mind. None of it matters now. You can forget what I said."

Suddenly it seemed to me he looked threatening, and to my own dismay I discovered that I felt frightened of him.

"I'm going home now," I said. "As I told you, you'd better go home too."

"I'm going."

I went to the front door. The last that I saw of him he was struggling into his leather jacket and adjusting a helmet on his head, getting ready, I supposed, to ride home on the motorcycle that I saw at the gate.

I found Felix in the kitchen, emptying a basket of things which he had bought that morning for our lunch, and perhaps for our dinner too. Sandra and Louella had gone, taking Jinks with them. Felix gave me a look of slight surprise when he saw me, and stopped digging anything more out of the basket.

"What's happened?" he asked. "You look queer."

"I've had a shock," I said.

"Over at the Creeds'?"

"Yes."

"Then come and sit down and tell me about it." He put an arm round my shoulders and guided me into the sitting-room. The fire had been lit and was crackling brightly. "Was the shock bad enough to need a whisky?"

I thought of Julia resisting the temptation to add gin to her orange juice because it was too early in the morning. But I decided it was foolish to let one's life be governed by the clock. After all, one only had to travel a short distance east or west to find that it was the clock itself that needed adjusting. Suppose I were in Australia at the moment, and if I shut my eyes I could pretend that I was, it would be sometime in the evening and certainly not too early for a drink. All the same, it is very difficult for a Briton to overcome years of conditioning that it is only proper to drink between certain hours.

"No," I said. Actually it had nothing to do with the time of day. I did not much want a drink.

"Then what's the trouble?" Felix asked.

"I just discovered that the people driving the Jaguar that you saw come away from the kerb here and that killed Malcolm were almost certainly Sue and Simon."

To my annoyance, Felix did not look as impressed as I had expected.

"I thought it was probably them," he said. "It seemed to make better sense than that it was the good doctor. How did you find it out?"

"Simon just told me." I had sat down near to the fire and begun to think that I would like some whisky after all. "As I told you, he's been over there this morning, looking after Julia, because his mother sent him. She herself left yesterday evening when she heard that her husband was being questioned about Sue's murder. And he started to say that he and Sue had been in to see Mrs. Bulpitt to tell her that they were going to get married, and then he suddenly got scared and said it happened some days ago. But I'm sure what he nearly said was that it had happened on Friday. And he asked me if I knew what Mrs. Bulpitt had done then, and I said no."

"Though you thought that you did."

"I don't really, Felix. It's what you did that I know about. But they thought it was her."

"You mean that telephone call of mine."

"Yes."

"Oh God," he said, "why did I ever do such a damn-fool thing? One ought never—I repeat, never—get involved in other people's problems. I was *not* blackmailing the doctor. You do understand that, don't you?"

The doorbell rang.

"Do you?" he said to me fiercely.

"Yes, of course. The bell, Felix . . ."

"All right, all right, I'm going."

"I know you've never quite blackmailed anyone."

"As long as that's understood . . ." He left the room and went to answer the door.

I was not expecting anyone in particular, unless perhaps the police once more. Expecting them was becoming a habit of mine. But when I saw Felix bring Godfrey Hamlyn into the room I felt as if I ought to have expected him to come sooner or later. It seemed improbable that he could just vanish from our lives without trace. There was some connection between us, if it was only that he must now be the owner of the house next door.

"I don't want to bother you, Mrs. Freer," he said as he sat down, "but I wonder if you would do me a favour?"

"If I can," I said. "But what about a drink?" I was quite sure that I wanted one after all. "Felix was just going to get me one."

"Me?" Felix said. "Yes—oh yes, of course. Sherry, whisky, gin, Hamlyn?"

"Gin and tonic, please, if you've got it," Godfrey Hamlyn replied, and Felix set about supplying him with it, while he poured out a strong whisky for me.

"It's just that I'd like to leave my address with you," Hamlyn went on. "Of course, the police have got it, but I'm going back to London this afternoon and staying there at least until the inquest, unless I'm wanted, and I'd like to know there's someone here who can get in touch with me if they see anything peculiar going on next door. Murder attracts people, as you probably know. Even on a miserable day like this there are people out there, gawping, and I'd sooner not have any uninvited intruders. The story may have got around about the missing thousand pounds and there might be some enterprising prospectors. If you'd just phone me if you see anything that worries you, I'd be very grateful."

"Do the police still know nothing about the thousand pounds?" I asked.

"No, except that they're fairly sure I took it, that's how it looks to me," Hamlyn said with a sardonic grin. "They couldn't be wider of the mark, of course. Since everything's coming to me anyhow, the thousand pounds would have come along with all the rest. Doesn't make sense, thinking I took it, does it?"

"And I suppose if Mrs. Bulpitt had simply given you the money, not expecting to be murdered, you could have said so," Felix said.

"Bless the old bitch, she'd never have done such a thing," Hamlyn replied. "Didn't I tell you that yesterday? I asked her if she could let me have some cash to help me out for the moment and she started to moan about how poor she was and how she hadn't anything to spare. And there she was with a thousand pounds in the house. Of course, I didn't know, any more than she did, that she was just going to be murdered, but once she had been I'd nothing to gain by taking the money. You know, it can't have happened more than ten minutes or so after I left the house. Now here's my address and telephone number." He took a wallet out of a pocket, extracted a card, and put it on the mantelpiece.

"Fact remains," he went on, "I'm suspect Number One. Not that they've put it in words so far, but I understood the drift of their questioning. They think my aunt gave me the thousand pounds, and when she'd done that, told me she'd made a will, leaving everything to me. So I'm supposed to have snatched up a hammer I saw in the kitchen, killed her, and forgot to put the thousand pounds back, which would have been the sensible thing to do. Or maybe not. Maybe I'm better off as I am, able to say I'd no possible motive for taking the thousand pounds. Maybe I was being very subtle."

The man finished his drink and stood up.

"But what motive do the police think you had for murdering Sue Lockett?" Felix asked.

"None that I know of, unless they believe those photographs I took of her prove we'd some sort of an affair going. Quite untrue. I believe myself the two murders have no connection with each other. It was just coincidence that they happened so close together. The girl was leading a sort of life that has its dangers. Now I'll be going."

He shook hands with me, then went out to the hall. I heard the front door close as Felix shut it after him.

He came back into the sitting-room.

"That thousand pounds," he said thoughtfully. "Of course he didn't take it."

"How d'you know that?" I asked.

"I suppose I'll have to tell you sooner or later," he said, reaching for a cigarette and lighting it as he gazed down thoughtfully into the fire. "You see, I took it myself."

NINE

FOR ONCE I did not doubt him. But I could not take it in.

"You stole that thousand pounds!" I exclaimed.

"No, certainly not," he said. "I did not steal it. I said I took it."

"What's the difference?"

"I took it, meaning to return it to its rightful owner."

I was hopelessly at sea. But that Felix should go so far as to steal a thousand pounds, as against a mere pair of pretty earrings, seemed so improbable that I was prepared to listen to some explanation of what he meant, even if it should turn out not quite to make sense.

"I told you about my phoning Gambrell," he said.

"Yes."

"And how I felt sure, when you told me about Mrs. Bulpitt getting that thousand pounds, that that was in response to what he thought was going to be blackmail."

"Yes."

"And how he was quite wrong, because I never meant him to do anything of the kind. I'd only been trying to check if the Jaguar was his and if it had been in Ellsworthy Street the night before."

"Yes," I said again.

"I hadn't thought out what I meant to do if I was right, and his sending the money meant of course that I was. It was a way of admitting that it was his car that killed Malcolm Creed, even if Gambrell himself wasn't driving it. I believed then that he had been, though I don't think so now, after what you've told me. But I thought it was quite wrong that he should be paying blackmail to someone who'd never asked for it and didn't even know what the money was for, and that it was all my fault. So I took it on myself to get the money back, meaning to return it to him."

"But how did you do it, Felix, and when?"

"I did it while Mrs. Bulpitt was at church and you'd gone off to your party. I'd seen her go out, so I knew the house was empty, and I went next door and let myself in—"

"Wait a minute!" I said sharply. "How did you get in? You hadn't a key."

"Oh, for God's sake!" he said. "Haven't I told you often that the sort of lock you've got on your door is simply an invitation to thieves? Any competent man could get in in a couple of minutes. Well, her lock is the same. I doubt if it took me as long as a couple of minutes to get in, then I prowled around for a little while, looking for somewhere she might have put the money. And my guess was that the kitchen was the probable place, and thought it might be in an empty tin or canister, as it was. It was in a canister labelled 'Coffee.' And I pocketed it, picked up the wrapping it had come in because I thought it might come in useful for making a parcel of the money to send back to Gambrell, and came back here. I thought I'd make up the parcel later in the day, because of course, being Sunday, there wasn't any hurry as I couldn't post it till next day. But before I got around to doing that we heard about the murder, and of course that upset everything."

"And where is the money now?" I asked. "Have you still got it?"

"Oh yes, it's in my suitcase."

"And what are you going to do with it?"

"That needs a little thinking about."

"You don't mean you're going to keep it!"

He hesitated for a moment, then said, "No—no, of course not."

"Why haven't you sent it back to Gambrell, as you say you meant to do?" I asked.

"Because, for one thing, I'm not sure it came from him."

I felt the sense of helplessness that I so often did in my dealings with Felix. It would really have been far easier for me if he had not had a conscience of any kind. But he had one, though it worked in a most mysterious way. I did not doubt for a moment that he had stolen the money from Mrs. Bulpitt because he had thought that it was his fault it had been mistakenly sent to her, and that it ought to be sent back to the man from whom it had come. Also I was sure that he was incapable of thinking of what he had done as stealing. But what did he really mean to do with it now?

"Why do you say the murder upset everything?" I asked. "Of course it upset all sorts of things, but why did it affect what you did with the money?"

"Think it out," he said. He lit a cigarette and sank into a chair. It struck me suddenly that he looked very tired. Perhaps some anxiety about his possession of the missing thousand pounds had been interfering with his sleep. "If I'd simply sent it to Gambrell *after* the murder, wouldn't he have concluded it came from the murderer, and if he'd told the police about it, wouldn't that only have confused them? Or just possibly, mightn't they have traced it back to me? Apart from fingerprints on the notes or the wrapping—incidentally I wasn't wearing gloves when I did the job, because I hadn't been expecting trouble, but I daresay there wouldn't have been any recognizable prints—but, as I said, apart from that, I'd have had to take it to the post office to send it to him, wouldn't I? And someone might have remembered that. Gambrell would have told the police the package came by post, and they'd have started some inquiries in local post offices, and quite soon they'd probably have got around to me, and might even have begun to think of me as the murderer."

"It would have been a rather strange murderer who posted his gains off to a complete stranger right after committing his crime," I said. "What possible motive could they have thought you had for the murder if it wasn't to get your hands on that money?"

"Suppose they thought I did it to protect you."

"Me!"

I was so startled that I jumped up from my chair and walked wildly about the room till I came to the window, when abruptly I stood still.

"Look!" I said. "Quick, come and look!"

Felix stood up and joined me at the window.

There was a police car outside the Creeds' house and I recognized the driver who was waiting in it as Jim Baker. The front door of the house was open and two men, one of them Sergeant Wells and the other unknown to me, were escorting Simon Prescott down the steps to the street. He was in his leather jacket, but was carrying his helmet. His motorcycle was where I had seen it when I left the house, though it was half hidden by the waiting police car.

It did not look to me as if Simon was under arrest. He had not been hand-cuffed, though the police presumably knew that he was a violent man. Their attitude to him appeared to be courteous. But I had never seen an arrest actually taking place and so did not know the meaning of what was happening on the other side of the street.

"The fools, the bloody fools!" Felix muttered. "I wish to God I knew what to do about it, Virginia. What do you think I ought to do?"

"Is there any need for you to do anything?" I asked. "They're probably just taking him in for questioning, as they did his father."

Simon and the two men got into the car and it drove away.

"But you see, I know who did it," Felix said.

I was not much inclined to believe him and I did want to know the explanation of what he had said a moment ago. I went back to my chair by the fire.

"Suppose we go back to your strange remark that the police might think you'd murdered Mrs. Bulpitt to protect me," I said.

He stayed at the window, looking out.

"Aren't you the only person who ever actually saw Mrs. Bulpitt get the thousand pounds?" he said.

"I don't see what that's got to do with it."

"Well, suppose they thought you'd taken the money from her, knocking her out with the hammer they found, but that you didn't really make a proper job of it, and when you came back and told me what you'd done I went round to make sure she wouldn't come round and accuse you of what you'd done, and finished her off. Then I sent the money back to Gambrell because I didn't want it traced to you."

"Far-fetched," I said. "You know this is the most complete nonsense you're talking. For one thing, the police would have found lots of people who saw Mrs. Bulpitt alive and well at church while I was at the Gleesons' party, and for another, would they have believed I could have been such a fool as to tell them about the money if I'd stolen it? So tell me your real reason for not sending it back to Gambrell. You said just now you weren't sure it had come from him."

"That only came later. This morning, to be exact, when your Sandra told us that Simon Prescott was Mrs. Gambrell's son. That changed my whole way of looking at the affair. I've already told you why I didn't send the money to Gambrell yesterday. It simply was because I was afraid I could be traced through my visit to a post office, if not as a murderer, then at least as a thief. But now that I know Prescott lived in the Gambrells' house, I've realised that it was almost certainly he and not Gambrell who answered my telephone call, and who somehow managed to get hold of that thousand pounds to send to Mrs. Bulpitt to stop her telling anyone that he'd been driving the car that killed Malcolm Creed. Doesn't that make better sense than that it was Gambrell who answered me? He didn't say, 'Dr. Gambrell speaking,' or anything like that, you know, as I ought to have expected. He only said, 'Yes?' Then as soon as I mentioned Ellsworthy Street he rang off. Oh—!" He stopped.

"What is it?" I said.

"You've got a visitor."

I turned my head and looked out of the window. Harriet Gambrell was coming quickly up the path to the house. In the road, nose to tail with Felix's car, was the silver-grey Jaguar.

She rang the bell, and as Felix did not seem inclined to move, I went to answer it. Without saying anything, almost as if she thought that I must know why she had come, she stepped in at the door. She was in a black suit, as elegant as the emerald-green dress in which I had seen her first, but her auburn hair looked as if a fierce wind had blown it into wild disorder, though there was no wind that morning. There was just the thin, steadily falling rain. Only frantic fingers could have brought it about.

As I shut the door, she gasped, "Isn't it terrible? Isn't it awful? You do know about it, don't you? Do you, Virginia?"

I took her arm and guided her into the sitting-room.

"You haven't met my husband, have you?" I said. "Felix, this is Mrs. Gambrell."

He advanced and held out his hand. She only gave him a puzzled glance, as if she could not imagine what he was doing there, limply took his hand, then dropped into a chair.

Ignoring him, she said to me, "Did you see anything? You're just across the street, you must have seen something. I expect everyone in the street was watching. But is it true that they've arrested him?"

"Simon?" I said. "I'm not sure. We saw the police take him away, but whether he's been charged with anything, or just taken to the police station for questioning, I simply don't know. How did you hear of it so soon?"

"I telephoned, you see," she said. "Only a few minutes ago. I wanted to ask him how he was managing and to tell him I could come back again and that he could leave. But it was Mrs. Creed who answered me and she said Simon had just been taken away by the police, so I jumped in the car and came round. I went to her house first, but she didn't answer when I rang, so I thought of coming here, to ask if you knew anything. But you say you don't know what's actually happened."

"Not beyond the fact that it's true they took him away," I said.

"And they're going to charge him with that girl's death, I know they are." There was a sob in her voice, though her eyes were wide and bright and tearless. "It's so horrible. He'd no reason to do anything like that. He was very fond of her. They were even thinking of getting married."

"So he told me," I said.

"Oh, you've seen him," she said, her voice suddenly sharp.

"Yes, I went over to see Mrs. Creed this morning," I said, "and he was there and we had a talk. I thought he was terribly upset about the girl's death. When I left he was crying his eyes out."

"Crying? Simon? I've never seen him cry since he was a little boy," she said.

"Well, he was crying this morning."

"And he said—what?"

"From what my wife's told me," Felix said, "nothing that you need be afraid of, Mrs. Gambrell. But I can't help wondering if those tears were really for the girl's death or for something much more difficult for him to face. I understand he was a violent young man, inclined to get into fights when he was drunk, but that doesn't mean he was used to the idea of having a violent mother. Now the question is, what are you going to do about it?"

Her body went rigid, then she gave a shudder that seemed to shake her from head to foot.

"What are you talking about?" she asked in a low, breathless voice, looking not at Felix, but intently, as if it hypnotized her, into the fire.

"Just asking what you're going to do about letting your son be arrested for what you did yourself," he said. "I do understand that it's a particularly difficult decision for you to make."

He sounded quiet, almost sympathetic, but there was something in his tone that made me want to shudder almost as Harriet had. It was partly shock, because I had not thought the matter out as he had, but also because I suddenly had the feeling, looking at Harriet, that there was something evil in the room, something that I would have recognized myself, if I had let myself do so.

"You don't know anything," she murmured into the fire. "You can't know anything."

"That's probably true," Felix agreed, "and luckily for me, it isn't my job to prove anything. But to go back to the beginning, your son and Sue Lockett paid a call on Mrs. Bulpitt on Friday evening, didn't they? And Simon was a bit drunk, not very steady on his feet. Perhaps Sue was too. They went in just to tell her that they were going to get married. Sue was one of the girls who'd been, as you might put it, on Mrs. Bulpitt's staff in London, wasn't she, and she seemed somehow to have kept a sort of regard for the old woman? Or was that call on her in reality a way of getting even? Did the girl want to tell her that in spite of what she'd done in the past, it was all over and done with and she was going to start a new life where Mrs. Bulpitt couldn't get at her? I don't suppose we'll ever know, unless your son tells us about it. They'd borrowed the Jaguar for the evening and left it parked outside Mrs. Bulpitt's house. And when they came out Sue got into the car and was followed by Simon, whom I saw just as I arrived here, though I didn't really notice anything about him except that he was staggering a bit, because the next thing I saw was that the car came swerving out from the kerb, knocked someone down, and drove straight on. And a moment later both Mrs. Bulpitt and my wife came running out of their doors, and then other people started coming. But of course Mrs. Bulpitt knew who'd been in the car."

Harriet looked up at him at last.

"And so?" she said. She sounded ironic, as if what he said meant very little to her.

"So that's where I come into the story," Felix said, "because as I arrived and saw the car go tearing off, I noticed some letters on its number-plate, and next day I saw the car in Durkin Square, in front of Dr. Gambrell's house. And I'm afraid I'm very much to blame for what happened next, because I wanted to check who the car belonged to, so I got the telephone number of Dr. Gambrell and rang him up. And someone answered. I took for granted it was Dr. Gambrell himself till I heard this morning that you'd a son living with you, and the fact that it was a man's voice that answered didn't necessarily mean it had been the doctor. I don't think now it was. I think it was your son. And the moment I said the words, 'Ellsworthy Street,' he simply rang off. But next morning, while my wife was with Mrs. Bulpitt, a package was delivered to her which contained a thousand pounds in ten-pound notes. Obviously, I thought, blackmail. Your son had taken my voice for that of Mrs. Bulpitt's nephew and thought pressure was going to be put on him because of his killing of Malcolm Creed. And he hoped a thousand pounds would buy her off."

Still watching him intently, Harriet gave a dry little laugh.

"How on earth do you think my son could have laid his hands on a thousand pounds?" she asked.

"From you, Mrs. Gambrell," Felix answered. "Didn't he tell you the whole story and didn't you give him all the money you could at short notice to take to Mrs. Bulpitt? I shouldn't be surprised if the police find you happened to have cashed a cheque for at least a thousand pounds on Friday or a day or two before, so you had that handy. And all would have been well if Mrs. Bulpitt hadn't been greedy."

I did not understand that. I said, "What do you mean, greedy, Felix?"

"She must have been, mustn't she?" he said. "Of course she guessed at once why and by whom that money had been sent, and if she'd been satisfied she'd be alive today. But the money coming like that put into her head the idea of what power she had over your son. She'd only to tell the police that he'd been visiting her, driving a Jaguar, on the Friday evening, and he'd have been arrested at once for manslaughter. So she rang up after my wife had left her and told you she wanted a good deal more than a thousand. And you came to see her. You'd been at a party with some people called Gleeson, and after it your husband had gone on to the hospital to have lunch with a colleague, while Sue and Simon were having lunch at the Rose and Crown. So it could only have been you. I don't know what you meant to do when you went to see her. Talk to her, reason with her, I don't know, but it didn't work and you lost your head. You were with her in the kitchen, I don't know why. Perhaps she was making coffee. She'd rather a passion for making coffee. And you'd followed her out and you saw the hammer in the tool-rack and—there you were."

She repeated the laugh of a few minutes before, though it sounded uneasier now.

"And you really think you've any proof of all this non-sense," she said.

"Oh no," Felix replied. "Next to none at all. But they've got your son, haven't they? I don't know how much that means to you, and what you do about it is of course up to you. I wouldn't try to advise you."

"You haven't explained how or why I murdered Sue," she said. Though her voice was calm, I thought it was with great difficulty that she was keeping it under control.

"The motive, I think, must have been the same as your motive for killing Mrs. Bulpitt," Felix answered. "The girl got greedy. She had been with Simon when he ran over Creed. She could always say that he'd been drunk when he did it and that she begged him to stop, but he wouldn't, and so put all the blame on him. And she probably knew the truth about the murder of Mrs. Bulpitt, as Simon certainly did. And she decided to put pressure on you for more money. So you somehow got hold of another blunt instrument—"

"The hammer!" I exclaimed. "The hammer that's missing from the Creeds' house. Of course it could only have been Simon or you who took it. No one else has been in the house."

"You haven't told me about that," Felix said.

"Julia told me the police had been to see her and had told her that Sue was killed by blows on the head with a hammer," I said. "And the hammer had Malcolm's fingerprints on it, and there used to be a hammer in a rack in their kitchen and it's missing now. And she couldn't tell them when it had disappeared."

Felix nodded gravely. "Yes, Mrs. Gambrell, that's fairly decisive, isn't it? It was Simon or you who took it."

"When am I supposed to have done this thing?" Harriet

asked. "I was with Mrs. Creed most of the day and with Simon in the Red Lion in the evening."

"After you'd picked Sue up in your car and killed her," Felix said, "I don't suppose you used the Jaguar. The traces of Sue that they found in it must have come from her trip in it on Friday evening. And Simon was only trying to help you set up an alibi. You'd dumped her body as quickly as you could, and it was sheer bad luck that it was found so promptly. The blood can hardly have been dry yet when they did. A shock for you. However, I've been told the second murder always comes more easily than the first."

Starting up suddenly from her chair, she screamed, "You devil!"

"I'm sorry," Felix said, and sounded as if he honestly meant it. "I really don't enjoy this sort of thing."

"There isn't a word of truth in what you've said!"

It was his fate, it seemed, never to be believed when he spoke the truth.

"Tell it to the police, tell it all, they won't believe you!" She swung round towards the door. The tone of her voice suggested that she might have been ordering him to tell it to the marines. "Good-bye, Virginia. I hope I never see you again."

She rushed out of the door. I sprang up from my chair, but I did not try to follow her. The front door slammed behind her and a moment later the Jaguar drove off.

I sank back into the chair from which I had started up.

"Whisky, please," I said.

Felix did not move towards the drinks cupboard. He remained where he was with a look of great pain on his face.

"I think I'm going to be sick," he said suddenly and hurried out of the room.

After a few minutes he returned, his face abnormally pale. "I'm not cut out for this sort of thing," he said. "I feel as if I've just murdered that woman myself. What was the evil chance that made me come here on Friday?"

"Chance is the word for it," I said. "Coincidence. Bad luck. Let's leave it at that. Perhaps it'll put you off coming here next Easter when Redgarth House opens again."

"Oh, I shan't be doing that anyway," he said. "There's a note about it in your local paper this morning. Abou Ben Adhem, may his tribe increase, has just presented his art collection to the nation and sold Redgarth House to a Swiss company who are going to turn it into a five-star hotel. So there won't be any job waiting for me here."

"Perhaps you might have some other reason for coming. Meanwhile, what about that whisky?"

He went to the cupboard, poured out a whisky for me and then, after a moment of uncertainty, one for himself.

I sipped mine and found it comforting.

"You know, you still haven't told me what you're going to do with that thousand pounds," I said.

"I don't know what to do with it, that's the truth," he said. "If I send it to Gambrell, it may lead to some very unpleasant questioning for me and perhaps even for you. If I send it in a plain cover to the police, they may try to nail Hamlyn for taking it. If he really had, he might return it to them out of fear that it would connect him with his aunt's murder. I can hardly send it to Mrs. Gambrell, though it might help a little with the costs of her defence. On the whole, I think the best thing to do with it might be to send it as an anonymous donation to Help in Need."

"Just so long as you don't forget you've got it and then happen to find it in a pocket in your suitcase a few weeks

from now, when the interest in the matter has rather sub-
sided."

"For God's sake, what d'you take me for?"

He knew only too well what I took him for, but I did not
pursue the subject.

"What do you think that woman will do now?" I asked.
"Will she let her son get a life sentence?"

"I don't put it beyond her," he said, "but I think, once the
police put some pressure on her, she'll crack. And if she
doesn't, Simon may. He's a tough enough character when it
comes to bashing Jim Baker on the jaw, but several hours of
steady questioning in a police station are rather different from
a brawl in a pub. Once the police have a fairly good idea of
what's happened, they'll get it out of one or the other of
them."

"But where are the police to get that pretty good idea
from?" I asked. "Are you going to see them now?"

"*I,*" he said in astonishment. "You'll do that, of course."

"Certainly not," I said. "The whole thing is your brain-
child."

He shook his head. "Not at all, Virginia. It was you who
knew about the missing hammer, wasn't it?"

"The police knew about that already," I said.

"But they've far more regard for you than for me," he
said. "I'm just someone passing through. You belong here.
And you're a friend of Jim Baker's. They'll take you seriously. Anyway, I'm leaving now. I'm sorry we've had such a
difficult few days together. I thought when I came that we
might be able to talk about—well, other things. But plainly
it wasn't the time for it. Some day perhaps we'll do that.
Good-bye now, my love."

He drank his whisky quickly, bent and kissed me on the

forehead, then went quickly out of the house to his car. He must have packed his suitcase earlier and put it in the car, ready for his departure, because he got straight into the car and drove away.

I did nothing for about half an hour except slowly sip my whisky. Great sadness always possessed me when I had just parted from Felix, though the feeling usually wore off fairly soon. Very reluctantly I eventually picked up the telephone. Dialling the police station, I asked for Detective Superintendent Dawnay . . .

I never inquired whether or not Help in Need ever received an anonymous donation of a thousand pounds, but perhaps they did.

ABOUT THE AUTHOR

E. X. Ferrars, who lives in England, is the author of over fifty works of mystery and suspense, including *A Murder Too Many* and *Trial by Fury*. She was recently given a special award by the British Crime Writers Association for continuing excellence in the mystery field.